Courtney ___ **s wail**
rose from ___

"Looks like we ___ time," she said. "Unless you want to volunteer for diaper duty…"

"No—no, that's all right," Travis stammered.

She hid a grin when he bolted for the door. As he neared it, his feet slowed and, along with them, so did her heart. At the last possible second, he turned around.

"We aren't done here, you and I." He wagged his finger between them. "I'll be by in the morning. We'll pick this up again."

Before she had a chance to disagree, he was out the door. As she watched his tall frame disappear down the street, she shook her head. In a coffee shop that would, hopefully, be filled with customers, there wouldn't be time to chat with a certain hunky baseball coach. No matter how much she wanted to. Or how often she told herself it was a bad idea.

Dear Reader,

When I was young, baseball was the only thing that tempted me away from the couch where I'd spend hours devouring one book after another. Our entire neighborhood turned out for Little League games, especially when the cute boy down the street pitched. Some of my fondest memories include sun-warmed wooden bleachers, popcorn and hot dogs from the snack bar, the sharp crack of a bat, cheering when "our" team won the game.

Former minor league pitcher Travis Oak shares my passion for baseball. Though he lost his chance to take the mound in the major leagues, he can't let go of the dream. Travis's life heads in a new direction when the Little League coach takes talented Josh Smith under his wing. A job that would be much easier if the boy's mom, Courtney, could admit why she hates the sport Travis loves. To earn her trust, Travis must convince the young widow he has her son's best interests in mind, even if he loses his heart in the process.

No author writes in a vacuum, and my special thanks go out to Dave Mastrolonardo for his insights into the life of a minor league baseball player. And to the members of Writers' Camp—the fabulous Roxanne St. Claire, the ubertalented Kristen Painter and the ever-encouraging Lara Santiago. We write at one another's dining room tables...and are thankful that you, our readers, enjoy the results.

I hope you like *Second Chance Family* and invite you to visit me at www.leighduncan.com and follow @LeighDuncan on Twitter.

Leigh Duncan

SECOND CHANCE FAMILY

—

LEIGH DUNCAN

HARLEQUIN® AMERICAN ROMANCE®

ISBN-13: 978-0-373-75509-7

SECOND CHANCE FAMILY

Copyright © 2014 by Linda Duke Duncan

Printed in U.S.A.

www.Harlequin.com

ABOUT THE AUTHOR

Award-winning author Leigh Duncan writes the kind of books she loves to read—ones where home, family and community are key to the happy endings everyone deserves. Married to the love of her life and mother of two wonderful young adults, Leigh lives on central Florida's east coast.

When she isn't busy working on her next story for Harlequin American Romance, Leigh loves nothing better than to curl up in her favorite chair with a cup of hot coffee and a great book. Follow Leigh on Facebook at LeighDuncanBooks, visit her website at www.leighduncan.com or drop her a line at P.O. Box 410787, Melbourne, FL 32941. She'd love to hear from you.

Books by Leigh Duncan

HARLEQUIN AMERICAN ROMANCE
1304—THE OFFICER'S GIRL
1360—THE DADDY CATCH
1406—RODEO DAUGHTER
1431—RANCHER'S SON

To my favorite baseball players

Joe, Bryan and Tyler

Chapter One

Travis Oak scouted the crowded hallway of Orange Blossom Elementary School. Shouts and laughter rose above the usual chatter of six hundred children moving between classes. He propped one shoulder against rose-colored concrete as Ms. Edwards opened the door to her sixth-grade classroom at the end of the hall. A new wave of kids surged toward him. A few students peeled off, headed for their next class. Others caught the scent of oven-fried chicken wafting from the cafeteria and quickened their steps. One familiar fresh-faced kid separated himself from the herd and approached.

"Hey, Coach Oak. What time are tryouts Saturday?"

"Nine o'clock, slugger." The search for a new team mom to handle the daily onslaught of questions from players and their parents moved up his priority list while Travis beamed a wide smile toward the returning pitcher on his Little League team. "All the information was in the packet your folks got when they signed you up this year. Have you been practicing those changeups like I showed you?"

"Yes, sir. When he gets home from work every night, my dad catches for me before we hit the batting cages."

Travis noted the slightest shift in twelve-year-old

Tommy Markham's brown eyes and knew the kid had just told a whopper. Oh, he had no doubt the boy practiced with his dad. Like most fathers, Thomas Markham Sr. had big-league dreams for his only son.

"You're not throwing that slider, are you?" he cautioned. When Tommy's face reddened, Travis ran a hand through hair he'd let grow a couple of inches now that he no longer spent twelve hours a day sweltering on a baseball field. In another year or two, Tommy's arm would grow strong enough to handle the hard snap required to send the ball spinning. Till then, throwing a curve was just asking for an injury.

"Listen to me, now," he said. "Concentrate on accuracy and speed. No curveballs till you're thirteen. Believe me, your elbow will thank you later."

"But, Coach, you should see the way the ball breaks away from the plate."

Remembering the sheer symmetry of throwing a perfect pitch, Travis let himself drift. He felt the cool white leather against his palm. His index finger sought the rippled edge of the seam. Arm up, his feet aligned with home plate, everything he had went into a powerful throw. A quick snap. The release. The follow-through. The ghost of a stitch in his side broke his concentration. He winced. Part of his job was to keep young players from hurting themselves.

"There's nothing prettier than a good curve. But you stick to fastballs and changeups or you'll ride the bench this season."

Tommy scuffed his shoe against the floor. "Yes, sir. See you at tryouts, Coach."

Travis watched until the boy merged with the rest of his sixth-grade pals and moved out of sight. The kid's big heart and love for the game made him any Little League coach's dream, but sooner or later Tommy and his dad would have to face the fact that Tom Jr. would be better off concentrating on his schoolwork. It took more than a strong arm and a good bat to make it to the pros.

Wasn't he living proof? He'd had both and had still never taken the mound in a major league park. Never heard the crowds roar his name on that long walk from the bullpen.

As the time for the next bell neared and the crowd thinned, Travis waved goodbye to Ms. Edwards. He made it halfway to the cafeteria before the pager at his hip squawked. Without breaking his stride, he grabbed the device.

"Oak here," he said into the mouthpiece.

"Mr. Oak, Ms. O'Donnell says there's a problem in the hallway outside her room." Static muffled the school secretary's voice. "Could you check it out?"

"Did she say what's up, Cheryl?" Travis stiffened. A *problem* could be anything from a bird in the hall to an armed intruder.

"A fight."

"I'm on my way."

Travis spun away from the lunchroom, his footsteps quickening as he headed for the far side of the school. He rounded a corner and stepped into Corridor C. On those rare occasions when he was called upon to break up a fight, one glimpse of his six-foot-two-inch frame headed their way usually sent the participants in opposite directions. Not this time. This time a ring of students surrounded flailing arms. Shouts rose above the hubbub.

"Hit him, Dylan. Hit him," chanted one of the hangers-on.

Travis picked up speed. "Make way, ladies and gentlemen."

The circle of students parted to let him through. He paused only long enough to assess the ineffective punches the two combatants traded before he stepped between them. Grabbing each boy by the shoulder, he firmed his voice. "Enough, gentlemen. That's enough."

Their fists still raised, the boys struggled against his grip. Travis recognized the larger one from sixth-grade Phys Ed and made eye contact. "Dylan Johnson. I said that's enough."

When Dylan's arms dropped to his sides, Travis turned his attention to the second boy. One glance at the blotchy red cheeks beneath a mop of shaggy blond hair told him Orange Blossom's newest fifth grader was still fighting mad.

"Son, enough already," he ordered the midyear-transfer student. So far neither of the boys had landed a single punch. If they kept it that way, he'd give them a stern talking-to and let them go.

"I'm not your son!" the kid let fly.

Travis barely suppressed a grunt when the wild blow caught him in ribs that occasionally sent up a flare three years after the break that had ended his own big-league dreams. Eyeing the new kid with a fresh measure of respect, he dredged up his best no-nonsense voice. "One more swing and you *both* go to Principal Morgan's office."

Fear and shame battled for first place in the hitter's blue eyes until, fists still clenched, the kid lowered his arms. The foes stepped farther apart, and Travis took a relieved breath. He didn't want to send these students to the office any more than they wanted to go. He turned toward the spectators.

"It's time for all of you to head for class or you'll be marked down as tardy."

The warning bell sounded through the corridor.

Spurred by the reminder of where they were and where they weren't supposed to be, kids scattered down the hall like leaves blown by a hard wind. In their wake, Dylan muttered something Travis didn't quite catch. With a yell, the new kid flew across the corridor. This time he landed a solid punch.

"Hey, slugger." Travis caught the boy's arm before he could draw it back again. "Were you trying to get into trouble? 'Cause you just bought the farm here."

"He said…he said…" The boy's mouth clamped shut.

Dylan broke in, his eyes tearing. "He's crazy, man!"

Travis eyed the scrappy fifth grader. A faded T-shirt hung from shoulders that were too wide for his thin chest. The frayed hem of his shorts brushed against sturdy legs. The rubber had separated from the sides of well-worn tennis shoes that Travis bet were at least a size too small. Despite himself, he gave the kid high marks for bravery. Not many would dare go up against an opponent a year older and twenty pounds heavier.

"What's your name?" he asked. He'd seen the boy around campus, but the kid hadn't dressed out for any of his P.E. classes.

"Josh. Josh Smith." The boy wiped his nose on his sleeve.

"Well, Josh, what seems to be the problem?"

Josh folded his arms across his chest. His lips thinned. "Ask him." He aimed his chin toward Dylan. "He started it."

"Uh-huh." Travis studied Dylan. Everything about

the sixth grader—from his all-too-familiar smirk to the way he leaned against the wall—told Travis the boy had stirred up this hornet's nest. "Dylan, what do you have to say?"

Dylan shrugged. "Nothin'. We were just talking about baseball and stuff. All of a sudden, he just went off on me."

Travis studied the two sullen faces. A bright red patch of skin below Dylan's eye was already starting to swell. The kid was going to have a shiner for sure. A shame because it meant Travis couldn't let either boy off with a warning.

"Okay." He let out a long breath. "Let's get you, Dylan, to the school nurse. Josh, you come with me to Principal Morgan's office."

"No fair!" Josh's eyes filled with fresh tears. "He started it. How come I'm the one who gets in trouble?"

Travis shook his head. "You're both in hot water. Dylan's the one with the black eye. He'll see the school nurse. You, my friend, will come with me."

"I am not your friend," Josh protested. "And I'm not your son, either."

"I'll keep that in mind." Travis nodded.

As he steered the boys toward the school office, he couldn't help but notice that beneath the hand he lightly placed on Josh's shoulder, the boy's hard muscles trembled. Travis felt a pang of regret, but the rules were clear. Fighting was not tolerated at OBE. The sooner Josh learned that, the better off he'd be. Once they dropped Dylan off at the infirmary, Travis left the fifth grader to cool his heels on a bench within sight of the secretary's desk. A quick nod guaranteed Cheryl would keep an eye on the boy. A purposeful look got Travis in to see the principal.

An old, familiar ache spread across his side as Travis folded himself onto a guest chair. He waited while Bob Morgan made a final notation on a report and pushed it to one side of his mahogany desk. Beneath a pair of sparse eyebrows, the principal's tired gray eyes sought his own.

"Don't ever go into administration," said his boss and former teammate. "The added paperwork and responsibility will make you old before your time."

"I hear you." Not that Travis needed the advice. Working with Little League and teaching physical education at Orange Blossom were only stopgap measures that kept his head in the game till he landed his dream job. He was on his way back to the pros, this time as a coach.

"So two of our young charges found an unacceptable way to settle their differences?"

Travis's mouth slanted to the side. "Yeah, unfortunately." He filled Bob in on the scant details. "Something about baseball. I was hoping to let them go with a warning, but Josh Smith landed a lucky punch."

Two, actually. He pressed a hand to his side. The kid packed a powerful wallop.

A concerned frown crossed Bob's face. "That makes the third scrape Josh has gotten into since he transferred at the start of the semester. The others weren't nearly as serious. I've talked with the boy, sent notes home, but he doesn't seem to be settling in here at Orange Blossom." Bob pressed a button on his intercom. "Cheryl, bring me the Smith boy's file. And call his mother. Ask her to come see me right away." When another light on his phone lit, he turned to Travis. "Sorry. That's the superintendent. Budget cuts—another wonderful part of my job."

Travis started to leave, but Bob waved him back into his chair, one hand cupped over the mouthpiece. "This won't take a minute."

By the time the secretary poked her head into the office, Bob had swiveled around so his back was to the door. Cheryl's gaze shifted from the principal to Travis.

"I'll take it," he said, reaching for the thin blue folder. He leafed past a request for records from Josh's previous school and stopped to read an initial evaluation that showed the boy lagged behind his classmates. The tutor who'd been assigned to help Josh catch up had opted the kid out of P.E. in favor of study hall, a move Travis suspected hadn't done the young boy any favors.

All that pent-up energy and no way to release it? That had to be tough.

While Bob continued his conversation, Travis turned to the personal-data sheet. Noticing that someone had scrawled "deceased" instead of filling in the blank with the name of Josh's dad, he frowned. He scanned the rest of the page, noting details that might explain the boy's failure to adjust to his new school.

Bob hung up the phone and leaned across his desk. "I take back what I said earlier about paperwork being the lousiest part of my job. Dealing with budget issues, that's worse. Then there's the joys of telling a parent you're going to expel their child. I don't look forward to the conversation with Ms. Smith."

Travis winced. Getting kicked out of Orange Blossom wouldn't solve any of Josh's problems. "Look." He tapped the file. "It says in here the boy's dad died in an automobile accident last year. Don't you think that explains the chip this kid is carrying around on his shoulders?"

Bob cupped his chin in his hand. "While that's probably the reason, our policy is clear."

"Even if he didn't start the fight? I'm pretty sure Dylan did that. He didn't deny it."

"So you think we should give Josh another chance?"

"I can't imagine what it's like to lose a parent, but I wasn't much older than this kid when my folks divorced." Travis gave his head a rueful shake. "That was hard enough. You know the trouble I got into till things settled out. Good thing I had baseball to ground me. Otherwise, who knows where I might have ended up. Josh doesn't even have that much. Heck, if it were me, I'd probably strike out at the world, too." His point made, he uncrossed his legs. Better minds than his would have to figure out Josh's future.

"So you have a plan for what to do with him?" Bob asked.

"Me?" Travis blinked. He was a P.E. teacher, not a principal. The kid wasn't his responsibility.

"You're the one who wants to keep him in school," Bob pointed out. "Come up with a plan to challenge him, or the next time he gets into a fight, I won't have a choice."

"When you put it that way…"

Travis leaned back to consider what little he knew about the boy. From Josh's ropy muscles and athletic build, it was clear the kid didn't sit around playing video games all day. And the fight had been about baseball, which proved the boy cared about the sport. The kernel of an idea began to take shape, and he nodded.

"Okay, how about we do this. Little League tryouts are Saturday. I'll draft him to my team, where I can help channel all that aggression into competition."

"That's a little outside the box, don't you think?"

Travis eyed the man who'd been his friend since they were Josh's age. Playing sports had gone a long way toward keeping them both on the straight and narrow.

"As I recall, you were quite the truant before Coach Marsden promised to kick you off the team if you skipped school one more time."

"Well, there is that. Little League, huh?" Bob rubbed his chin. "I guess we can give it a try, as long as Josh and his mom agree."

"Hah," Travis scoffed. Of course the mom would say yes. What parent didn't want a former minor league baseball player as their son's Little League coach? Not only did he have an eye for talent, but experience had taught him how to bring out the best in the boys. His team had won the district play-offs last year. Since most of his best players would return again this season, he hoped to go even further. State. Maybe even regionals.

Bob cleared his throat, and the image of a championship trophy winked out.

"You know how I hate giving up on a child. Especially when there are extenuating circumstances, like a death in the family. But, Travis, there can't be any more fighting at school."

Travis rubbed his sore ribs. No more fights was fine with him, too.

IN THE BACK office of Coffee on Brevard, Courtney Smith stared down at one-year-old Addie. Though she stirred restlessly in the portable crib, her daughter had fallen asleep.

"Finally," Courtney whispered. She wrangled loose

strands of her shoulder-length hair into a ponytail, wound it into a knot and anchored it in place.

A new tooth had spelled sore gums and extraordinary fussiness for her daughter. It had turned the day into one of those rare occasions when Courtney wished she could still hand a crying baby off to a nanny.

She shook her head. The times when someone else took care of her children, when she spent her mornings at the spa and her afternoons at the ballpark, when every detail of her life was determined by how it impacted her husband's career—those days were over. As were the countless tears she'd shed both before and in the nine months since the accident that had changed everything.

She gave her hair a final pat. It was time to move on. Time to build a future for herself and for her children.

Not that she was ready to forgive Ryan for the way he'd destroyed their lives, but she'd gladly traded the social whirlwind that had enveloped her as the wife of a major league baseball star for the peace, quiet and anonymity offered by Cocoa Village. Sure, there were things she missed about their old life. She held up one hand, her fingers spread. She'd give her eyeteeth for a manicure. But what use were weekly trips to the nail salon if the polish chipped off the first time she scrubbed out a coffeepot?

Which, she reminded herself, she'd better get busy doing if she was going to keep a roof over their heads. Addie's crankiness had put her behind schedule. She slipped the baby monitor into her pocket and quietly stepped from her office.

In the dining area, she swept an appraising glance over the café. Turning the vacant storefront into a welcoming oasis had been a huge risk, but the results were everything she'd hoped for. White trim above pink-and-green-striped wallpaper gave the room a cheery Florida look that balanced nicely against the dark green wainscoting. Glass droplights illuminated each of the small tables she'd dressed with starched linens and fresh flowers. Hardwood floors added to the ambiance. Best of all was the nook she'd created in one corner. There she encouraged patrons to take one of the current bestsellers from her small collection and curl up on the comfy sofa, a novel in one hand, a steaming cup of coffee in the other.

Now, if she could only drum up enough business to stay afloat, she'd be okay.

She worried a thumbnail. Building a loyal clientele took time. At least, that was what all her college professors had taught. And she was making progress. Only two months after she'd opened the doors to Coffee on Brevard, business had grown from the occasional customer to a steady trickle. It wasn't enough to make ends meet yet—not quite—but if people liked the soup-and-sandwich special she'd added to the lunch menu, she could squash the fear that kept her up at night. The one where she ended up living out of her car with two kids and no prospects.

She hurried to the tall granite-topped counter at the front of the café. Stepping behind it, she stirred the simmering pot of soup she'd started before Josh left for school. The smell of cream of asparagus mingled pleasantly with the house blend and the vanilla almond that was today's special coffee.

Across Brevard Avenue two shoppers emerged from one of the gift shops along the village's main thoroughfare. Bulging bags hung from their arms. From their high-end footwear to their carefully tousled hairstyles,

Courtney knew them. Oh, not their names or how their husbands earned a living, but she recognized their type. A year ago she'd lived a life very much like theirs. But hers had come at too great a price.

She took a deep breath. The past was behind her. Today she needed to focus on whether the warm February weather would draw the shoppers and others into her café.

Banking on it, Courtney opened three large cans of solid white albacore and spooned the expensive tuna into a colander. Within minutes she'd chopped hard-boiled eggs and finely diced enough celery to triple her grandmother's recipe. She'd measured out the requisite amount of mayonnaise when the phone rang. She scooped it up, her smile fading when she recognized the number on the caller ID.

"Coffee on Brevard. This is Courtney." She mustered a businesslike tone. Slowly, she lowered the jar of mayonnaise to the counter, her concern for her son on the rise. Would her ten-year-old ever adjust to his new school…or forgive her for spiriting him away from their old life in Orlando? She crossed her fingers and hoped his teacher had called with good news about Josh's grades.

"Ms. Smith, this is Cheryl Lewis, the secretary at Orange Blossom."

Courtney froze. The phone wedged between her chin and her shoulder, she braced for worse news than a failed spelling test. "Yes, Ms. Lewis?"

"Ms. Smith, I'm afraid there's been a problem. Principal Morgan would like you to come to the school as soon as possible."

A lump formed in Courtney's throat. "Is…is Josh all right?"

"He was in a fight." Disapproval weighted the answer. "Can you come right away?"

Panic rose at the possibility that her only son had been hurt so soon after the accident that had ripped their lives apart.

"I'm on my way." With shaking hands, she hung up the phone.

After shutting off the flame under the soup, she double-timed it to the back room, where she scooped up a sleeping Addie, flung the diaper bag over one shoulder and grabbed her purse. Back through the shop she ran. She paused only long enough to flip the Open sign to Closed before she stepped onto the sidewalk and keyed the dead bolt.

Fifteen minutes later Courtney pulled into a crowded parking lot, grabbed Addie from the backseat and darted into the school. She stepped into the administration office while her pulse hammered against her temples. Immediately, she spotted Josh slumped on a bench beneath a colorful mural. He didn't look hurt. Angry, maybe. But not hurt.

Relief brought tears to her eyes. On legs that trembled so much she wasn't sure how they supported her, she crossed the tile floor to her son. A torrent of questions filled her mind.

Powerless against them, she asked, "Josh, honey, what happened? Were you in a fight? Are you okay?"

At the sound of her voice, her ten-year-old sat up straight. His arms crossed. In the accusatory tone he'd perfected in the months since his father's death, he demanded, "Why did you have to come?"

Courtney stared into her son's hooded blue eyes and felt her heart lurch. Ever since the night they'd lost Ryan, she'd been afraid of losing her little boy, too. She'd let Josh think it was her idea to start a new life in Cocoa Village. He believed she'd chosen to end their long afternoons at the ballpark where the Smith family received the royal treatment. That she'd wanted to move out of their house, leaving his toys, his friends, behind.

He'd learn the whole sordid story sooner or later. In fact, she suspected Josh already knew more than either one of them wanted to admit. But until the truth came out, at least they were together. They still loved each other. They were a family.

Couldn't he see that?

Not if the scowl he wore was any indication.

At her hip, Addie stirred and began to whimper. Courtney grimaced. One unhappy child at a time was all she could handle.

"Shh, baby girl," she soothed.

She needn't have worried. Addie's bright blue eyes latched on to the colorful wall above Josh's head. The little girl pointed. "Burr."

Courtney spared a single glance at the large pink flamingo that was OBE's mascot. "That's right. Bird," she confirmed while her daughter cooed delightedly. With Addie occupied, she faced her son, intent on getting some answers no matter how angry he was.

On the other side of a low counter that separated the waiting area from the offices behind it, the school secretary called, "Ms. Smith, Principal Morgan will see you now."

"I'll be right there," Courtney answered, her focus still on Josh. "We'll talk this evening," she promised, her tone letting her son know that while she acknowledged his pain, he still had to follow the rules.

His face crumpled. "I'm sorry, Mom. I didn't start it. Honest, I didn't."

At the plea for forgiveness, Courtney fought an urge to drop to her knees and pull her little boy into her arms. She settled for ruffling the thick blond hair that was so much like his dad's.

"Thanks, Josh," she said. "That's really good to hear."

Maybe there was hope after all. Maybe she could turn her fledgling coffee shop into a thriving business. Maybe she could help Josh let go of the past to become the sweet, lovable child he'd been until his father died. Maybe she could be a good enough parent to make up for the fact that neither of her children would ever have a dad.

Maybe. But it was far more likely that all her dreams would come crashing down around her.

While Addie squirmed and jabbed her stubby fingers toward the pink flamingo, Courtney drew in a deep breath. She marched past the counter to the office marked Robert Morgan, Principal. Resettling the baby on her hip, Courtney couldn't deny the feeling that she, more than her son, was in trouble.

"I counted ten scouts at the district tournament last year. One was a buddy of mine, Frank Booker. He's pretty high up in the Norfolk organization."

Travis leaned back in his chair. Though the Sluggers had done well, the scouts had shown more interest in him than in his players. The next time the Norfolk Cannons had an opening for an assistant coach, Travis's name was at the top of a very short list of candidates. A fact Frank had confirmed over their third beer.

"Do you miss it? Playing ball?" Bob asked.

Like I'd miss my right arm.

Nothing compared to the exhilaration he felt when he struck out the other team's ace—a feeling he hoped to rekindle when he coached rookie players in the pros.

Guessing that wasn't what his old friend wanted to hear, Travis gave a different version of the truth. "Some aspects more than others."

Of course, playing in the minor leagues had its drawbacks. Like the nights he'd spent trying to catch some shut-eye on a bus filled with guys just as anxious to make it to the next level. A low hum stopped him before he could confess how much he enjoyed waking up in his own room every morning, even if he hadn't found anyone special enough to share his king-size bed.

Bob held up a finger. "Hold that thought," he said, and told Cheryl to admit their guest. To Travis he added, "Showtime."

While the man in charge leafed through Josh's file, Travis straightened out of the relaxed pose he'd adopted during the twenty-minute discussion of his favorite sport. His focus shifted to the closed door, his expression hardening into his game face.

He wasn't sure what he expected, but the slim, petite blonde who entered the room with a baby on one hip and desperation in her sad blue eyes certainly wasn't it. With her thick blond hair captured in a simple bun and her face devoid of makeup, Ms. Smith looked far too young to be the mother of a ten-year-old. Curious, Travis scrutinized the woman, whose blouse nipped in neatly at her waist. Aware that he was staring, he forced his gaze to a pair of slender feet in sturdy loafers that were anything but elegant.

The baby in her arms stirred, and she absently patted its diapered bottom.

"Hush, now, Addie," she whispered.

Travis tossed his interest to the side the same way he used to discard a bat after getting a hit. A widow with a baby and a difficult preteen presented too many challenges for a guy with his sights set on coaching in the big leagues. He quashed the faintest glimmer of attraction to Ms. Smith with a stern reminder that he was here only to help her son. Yet he couldn't completely ignore her large eyes, where sorrow and fear shone like beacons.

Bob Morgan rose to greet his guest. "Ms. Smith, thanks for coming in."

"Courtney, please." She extended one hand across the desk.

Shaking the proffered fingers, Bob said, "I'm sorry we have to meet under these circumstances."

Courtney Smith's chin trembled. "I've spoken with Josh. I don't think he was injured. Was the other child hurt?"

Travis aimed a raised eyebrow at Bob. Most parents were so busy making excuses for their own children they didn't spend a minute worrying about anyone else's.

Bob cleared his throat. "The school nurse says, other than an impressive shiner, Dylan will be fine."

Courtney blinked away the tears that shimmered in her eyes. "I'm very sorry for Josh's behavior. I'm sure he'll tell you the same thing. Do you know what started the fight?"

"Coach Oak here was the one who intervened. Travis, why don't you tell her what you told me."

At Bob's signal Travis rose. He gave the brim of his baseball hat a tug. "Ms. Smith," he said, aiming a wide smile in her direction. An effort that apparently had no effect on Josh's mom. He chalked her grudging "Courtney" up to a mild irritation at having to repeat herself and plunged into the task he'd been given.

"Neither boy would say much," he admitted. "From the little I was able to piece together, it had something to do with baseball."

The baby in her arms whimpered, and Courtney's posture slumped. Without a word, she reached into the big bag that hung from one shoulder and came up with a bottle. Bob waited until she cradled the little one before he launched into a review of the school's no-fighting policy.

Travis only half listened, his attention riveted on the slim blonde, who said "Yes" and "I understand" in all the right places without glancing up from the baby. He frowned, recalling one of a thousand nights when his own mom had juggled his demands as well as his brother's while she set dinner on the table. He made a mental note to send her some flowers. Raising two boys without help had to have been harder than he'd ever imagined, but at least their dad had waited until he and Cal were in their teens before he'd split. The challenges Courtney Smith faced in trying to care for a baby and a young son had to be much worse. An urge to help her and her boy stirred in his chest and he smiled, glad he'd found a way to do that.

"I understand what a tough year this has been," Bob said at last. Sympathy clouded his eyes. "For you and the rest of your family. Ordinarily, I'd expel Josh, but Coach Oak has come up with a solution we think will help your son stay in school."

At his cue Travis summoned his most disarming smile.

"Courtney." He paused, half expecting the flicker of interest he usually got from members of the opposite sex.

His self-confidence took a small hit when the prettiest
pair of blue eyes he'd seen in a long time remained indifferent. He countered her reaction with a quick reminder
that his plans for the future didn't include a single mom
with two children.

Back on track, he continued, "I understand that Josh's
old school didn't have the same high expectations for its
students that we require here at OBE, so he meets with
a tutor instead of taking Phys Ed."

In an oddly endearing move, Courtney tugged her bottom lip between even white teeth. She nodded.

"Now, I wouldn't dare suggest we change that." Out of
the corner of one eye, he aimed a pointed glance toward
the principal. Academics always came first at Orange
Blossom. "But I'm sure you're aware of how important
exercise and sports are for growing youngsters. Your son
apparently has quite the passion for baseball. I'd like a
chance to see if I can channel it into something that won't
get him into so much trouble."

He'd have sworn he caught Courtney's attention when
he mentioned the game in which he'd spent his life trying to excel. Taking her reaction as a good sign, he carried on. "Little League tryouts are this weekend. If you'll
make sure Josh is there, I'll draft him to my team, the
Sluggers. The sportsmanship and camaraderie he'll learn
this season will go a long way toward turning around
his attitude."

He frowned when Courtney shook her head.

"Baseball?" Her eyes darkened. "Thanks, Coach. But
no thanks."

Travis fought the urge to scratch his head. What could
the woman possibly have against baseball? He started to
argue, but Bob beat him to the punch.

"Now, Ms. Smith, I can assure you that Coach Oak will take good care of your son. I've known him most of his life, and though this is only his third year at OBE, he's already earned the respect of our entire school and community. He's great at encouraging young boys to achieve their potential. No one in Cocoa Village knows more about baseball than he does. Why, he'd be pitching for the Norfolk Cannons right now if he hadn't broken a couple of ribs his last year in the minors."

Bob made such a good wingman that Travis promised to buy the man a beer the next time the teaching staff met for happy hour. But enough was enough. He held up a hand to stop the flow of compliments and get the focus back where it belonged, on Josh. He glanced at Courtney Smith, hoping the principal had made the right impression.

"Josh doesn't play organized sports," she coolly insisted. She stared at Travis as if he had the plague. "And he most assuredly does not play—" her lips formed what looked an awful lot like a sneer "—baseball."

Never? Never played catch? Never ran around the bases?

Travis clenched his teeth. Every one of his returning players had started with T-ball when they were six, followed by two or three years in the lower levels before he drafted them. Josh Smith would fit in with them like a fish out of water. He opened his mouth to tell Bob he'd changed his mind about putting the boy on his team. One look at Courtney's pale face renewed his resolve to do what was right by her son.

"Last year my Little League team won the district tournament. We're hoping to do even better this year. That might be harder to accomplish if I draft such an inexperienced player." He paused, giving the single mom a chance to appreciate the sacrifice everyone was making for her boy. "But I believe baseball will give Josh's passion for the game a healthy outlet. From what I've seen, he's a sturdy little scrapper. Who knows?" he asked, prepared to dangle the carrot every parent wanted for their child. "He might just be a superstar waiting to be discovered."

From the color that filled Courtney's cheeks, Travis knew he'd scored a home run. He studied her, waiting for the effusive thanks that came whenever he chose a boy for his team.

Courtney's lips firmed. Her shoulders straightened. Travis swore the temperature in the room dropped when she pinned him with an icy stare.

"Absolutely not," she issued through clenched teeth. "I will not allow my son to have anything to do with Little League. Or with you."

In her arms, the baby wailed.

Chapter Two

Courtney stared into the silence that filled the office. Behind a scarred mahogany desk, Principal Morgan's brows hovered above disbelieving eyes. As for the big hunk in the corner, Travis Oak looked for all the world like a batter who'd taken one for the team and was trying hard to hide how much it stung. Which served him right for being so… She flipped through descriptions and frowned at the adjectives that tickled her tongue. A second glance was definitely in order.

From broad shoulders to muscular legs, everything about the coach said he was a take-charge, winning kind of guy. The kind of man other men respected. The kind who'd grown used to having flirty women agree with everything he said.

Good-looking?

Yes, she'd give him that. From the thick dark hair that brushed the collar of the T-shirt stretched across his chest to the powerful thighs that made even a baggy pair of sweats look good, the man made quite the impression. Beneath the brim of a baseball cap, the tanned planes of his face sloped down to a chiseled jaw. She placed him somewhere in his mid-thirties despite the full lips that gave him a more youthful appearance. Tiny lines at the corners of deep-set brown eyes hinted at a wisdom beyond his years.

If he were simply a teacher, she'd have appreciated his interest in her son. If he taught history or English or math, she would have asked him if he tutored. But she couldn't argue with the facts. And the fact was, Travis Oak had struck out.

The man had played professional baseball. Strike one.

He coached a championship Little League team. Strike two.

Having failed in his own quest to reach the major leagues, he was on the hunt for a kid who might go all the way. *Strike three, and you're outta here.*

Baseball had already stolen her husband, robbed her children of their father, left her little family to face an uncertain future. She refused to let it ruin her son's life, too.

"Excuse me, but, I don't think you understand." Principal Morgan broke the silence.

"What's difficult about it?" Courtney shrugged. "I won't let Josh play Little League. Or any other organized sport." She summoned all her bravado. "Especially not with a minor league player as his coach."

Travis folded his arms across a chest so wide it dwarfed the school mascot on his T-shirt. "Are you saying I'm not good enou—"

Save me from athletes and their fragile egos.

"No, it's not that at all," Courtney said with a sigh. "I'm sure you're a fine coach." Framed certificates for innovative leadership crowded the walls of the principal's office. "There has to be another answer."

The man in charge cleared his throat. "Ms. Smith, our rules are clear. I'm bending them to make an exception because your son is new to our school. But I'm afraid this is Josh's only chance. If you don't go along with this plan, I will expel him."

Courtney bristled. The principal was wrong about her son. Josh wasn't a bad kid. He certainly didn't deserve to get kicked out of school. Sure, he'd had some problems. He'd missed so much class work last year that he'd fallen behind. In his struggle to accept all the changes in his life, he'd sassed his teacher, shown up late for class. Those had cost him his television privileges for a month. Still, given all he'd been through, a little bit of acting out was to be expected, wasn't it? If Principal Morgan only knew the real reason…

She stopped herself.

He didn't know. No one did.

A year ago she'd been the wife of *the* Ryan Smith. Her children had lived a fairy-tale existence. She ran a hand over the simple updo she'd adopted shortly after discovering there'd be no more expensive salon trips in her future. Amazed that she'd once squandered money at Saks when the clothes she bought off the clearance rack at Walmart were just as good, she gave the hem of her shirt a tug. Okay, there was still one pair of to-die-for heels in the back of her closet, but other than those, she'd traded in her Jimmy Choo shoes for serviceable footwear.

Was it any wonder that no one in Cocoa Village had made the connection between a widow determined to eke out a living for her two kids and the wife of a superstar?

Eventually the truth would come out. She cringed at the thought of what would happen when it did. After the car accident, the paparazzi had trailed her home from the hospital. Reporters from all over the globe had camped out on the front lawn. In their quest for a story—any story—about baseball's number one bad boy, reporters had held her up for public ridicule. Blamed her for Ryan's philandering ways, his drug use, his gambling. They'd publicized every move she or her children made until she'd loaded what was left of her family into a five-year-old sedan—the only vehicle she could still afford—and escaped in the dead of the night.

She couldn't put Josh through that notoriety again. Not until he adjusted to their new life. Not before the business she'd started with the last of the money she'd scraped together was solidly in the black. Until then she had to keep their past a secret. For her son's sake more than for her own.

Morgan tapped a pen against his desk. "You have options. There are several private schools in the area."

"I can't afford the tuition," she objected. Her checking account was already on life support.

"You could homeschool."

At her frown, the principal showed her his palms.

"Or there's the Alternative Learning Center."

"That's for juvenile delinquents." She felt the color drain from her face.

"That's all I have to offer, Ms. Smith."

She risked another glance at the coach, her quick study catching a glimmer of awareness in his brown eyes. If there was one thing she knew about men who earned their living on a ball field, it was their win-at-all-costs attitude. As a professional athlete, even a former one, Travis Oak was her best ally in keeping Josh off his team.

She steered her attention to the principal. "So you're saying if Josh shows up for tryouts, you'll let him come back to school?"

"No, Ms. Smith, I'm saying he has to play the entire season for Coach Oak."

"And if he isn't good enough to make the team?" Though Ryan's record would one day earn him a place in the Hall of Fame, no one had ever awarded him a medal in fatherhood. He and Josh had never played catch in the backyard. Baseball's greatest hitter hadn't even taught his son how to swing a bat. The idea that Travis would want her boy on his championship team was ludicrous.

"I'll draft him no matter what." From his corner Travis's deep voice filled the room. "You have my word on that."

Convinced she hadn't misjudged his competitive nature, Courtney faced him.

"Are you sure? If I remember the rules, every kid on your team has to actually play in every game."

"So you know a thing or two about baseball." Travis's lips curved into a perceptive smile. "You just don't want your son to play the game."

She flinched as his remark struck too close to the truth. Determined not to let him affect her, she dug deep for a scathing retort that died on her lips the instant their eyes met. For a second, she froze, unable to look away no matter how much she told herself she wanted to. An emotion she couldn't quite identify flared in Travis's dark eyes, and this time she did step back.

When the pen Bob Morgan had been holding fell to his desk with a clatter, she used the excuse to draw away from Travis's intense gaze. Maybe he thought he understood her plight. Maybe he was just being neighborly by helping out the new widow in town. Whatever his intentions, it didn't matter. She'd keep her distance.

"Ms. Smith?" The principal cleared his throat. "What's it going to be? Expulsion? Or Little League?"

Her stomach quivered. How was she supposed to

choose? "I need to think about it. Whatever I decide, I have to discuss it with my son."

Neither man put any effort into masking his disappointment, but Principal Morgan spoke.

"This is Thursday. I can hold off putting the paperwork through until Monday. In the meantime, Josh is suspended. If he shows up at tryouts, he can return to school next week. If he doesn't, no matter what the excuse—" the principal pinned her with a look that was all business "—I will expel him."

"I understand." She nodded. Removing the bottle from Addie's mouth, she hoisted the baby to her shoulder. She aimed a final caustic look at the coach, who'd placed her squarely between one terrible choice and a worse one, and gathered her dignity for the long walk out of the room.

As soon as she stepped into the outer office, Addie started to babble. "Burr! Osh!" She pointed toward her brother. "Osh! Burr!"

"Hush, Addie," Courtney whispered. She might as well have been talking to a wall. Her daughter's chatter only grew louder. Without taking her eyes off her son, Courtney made her way past the reception counter to his side.

Josh scrambled to his feet. "What'd Principal Morgan say, Mom? Did you tell him I was sorry? I won't get in any more fights."

She took one look at the hopeful expression on his face and straightened her shoulders. Parenthood was definitely not for the faint of heart.

"Josh, get your things together. We're going home," she said, unwilling to discuss matters where others might overhear. Confusion muddied the blue eyes that stared up at her.

Josh tilted his head to one side. "But I haven't had lunch. I'll miss music class this afternoon."

Courtney swallowed. "I know. But you can't stay here, so we have to go home. Now. I'll explain more later."

Seeing tears well in his eyes, she fought to stay calm. His wasn't the only day that hadn't gone according to plan. She was supposed to be behind the counter at Coffee on Brevard, serving up a cheery smile to go along with soup, sandwiches and coffee. Instead, she'd lost business she couldn't afford to lose. To make matters worse, her only hope of keeping her son in school was to let him participate in the very sport she'd sworn she'd never have anything to do with again.

She ached to tell Josh everything would be okay, but how could she when she wasn't sure herself?

TRAVIS FOUGHT A desire to stare after the slim young woman as she marched out of the room. He lost the battle. A low whistle escaped his lips.

"Well, that certainly didn't go the way I expected." Bob's chair squeaked as he leaned away from his desk. "Do you and Ms. Smith have a history I should know about?"

Travis removed his baseball hat and ran a hand through his hair. His fingers came away surprisingly damp. He rubbed them together, chalking the moisture up to a higher-than-normal humidity level. Courtney Smith certainly didn't have a thing to do with it. He shook his head.

"Never seen her before in my life." But there was no denying that something had put him squarely on her bad side. He couldn't remember the last time he'd been shot down. He was pretty sure no one had ever done it with such finality. Except for the tiniest spark when their eyes met, the woman hadn't shown so much as a flicker of interest. Not even his success in the minor leagues had impressed her. If anything, he suspected his history in pro ball had worked against him.

Which made her one in a million, whether hers was the most common last name in America or not.

True, he'd never made it to the majors, but there'd been a time when a raised eyebrow was all it would have taken to summon something soft and willing to his bed. Back in those days, when he'd refused to get involved with the cleat chasers who filled the bars after a game, his team-mates had practically labeled him a monk. He'd put up with their gibes because, having come from a broken home, he knew how it affected a kid. Vowing he'd never put a child of his own through that, he'd set his standards impossibly high. While that meant spending his nights alone, it was a trade-off he'd been willing to make.

Lately, though, as he'd watched fellow teachers and former teammates with their families, he'd begun to wonder if he'd ever find the right woman.

Courtney Smith, with her petite frame and a keen wit that showed itself despite her literally getting called to the principal's office—now, there was a woman who might meet his criteria. A man could get lost in those big blue eyes. She had the perfect amount of curves in all the right places. He shifted uncomfortably at the thought of her golden hair cascading softly around her shoulders. If she'd shown the slightest indication that she felt the same way about him, he might have asked her out.

If it weren't for a couple of big stumbling blocks. As for those...

Despite himself, he stared out the door as Courtney settled the baby—Stumbling Block #1—on her hip. She placed a gentle hand on the shoulder of Stumbling Block #2. The kid gave her an incredulous look and jerked away.

Travis took in a deep breath. If there was ever a woman who needed help, Courtney did. Yet she'd rejected his offer before she could even hear him out. It wasn't as if he'd tried to seduce her. As tempting as that idea might be, he'd simply wanted to help her son.

What widow with two kids wouldn't appreciate the gesture?

He waited until she disappeared through the main door before he succumbed to a growing need for more information. "What do you know about her?"

"Not much," Bob answered with a shrug. "According to Josh's records, she and the children are new in town. She opened that coffee shop in Cocoa Village a couple of months ago. I haven't been there, but my wife says it's fixed up real nice inside." Bob nodded to himself. "Small place like that, she probably manages it all by herself."

"I imagine so," Travis agreed. He put himself in her situation and felt a little sick to his stomach. He pushed aside the stab of sympathy. "I have to get to my next class," he said, standing.

"Let me know how it goes Saturday. I'm sure once she thinks about it, Ms. Smith will realize that playing Little League is the best solution for her boy."

"I wouldn't bet on it." Travis's mouth slanted to one side.

The doubt in Bob's eyes shifted suggestively. "I've

seen the way you operate, Travis. There isn't a woman
on our staff you haven't got wrapped around your little finger, including Cheryl there." He nodded toward
the white-haired secretary who manned the front desk.
"If you really want to help this boy, you might consider
swinging by a certain coffee shop after school. Pour on
a little charm. Ms. Smith won't be able to resist. Who
knows where that might lead?"

"I admit, I've got a sudden hankering for caffeine."
Travis flashed a quick grin on his way out the door. "I'd
like to put Josh on my team, see if we can't work on his
attitude a bit. As for his mom, though…she's definitely
not my type."

Courtney Smith might have cornered the market on
gorgeous, and her willingness to stand up to him was
refreshing. But a guy intent on coaching in the pros
couldn't afford a needy woman in his life. A young
widow single-handedly raising a baby plus a kid with a
Mount Rushmore–size chip on his shoulder? Well, that
situation had *need* written all over it.

"CAN I GO to the park, Mom?"

Are you nuts, kiddo?

Courtney awarded herself a gold star in parenthood
when she refrained from asking the question. Shaded
by enough trees to keep children cool through the dog
days of summer, the city park was filled with swings and
slides. It was also two blocks away, and Josh knew he
was never allowed to go there by himself. Plus, he was
in trouble with a capital *T*.

Without saying a word, Courtney parked behind Coffee on Brevard. She counted to five before she propped

one arm over the seatback. She turned, prepared to explain in no uncertain terms that Josh was grounded.

No trips to the park. No video games. No television. Maybe for the rest of his life.

One glimpse of the clear blue eyes that bore no sign of the surly attitude she'd come to expect from her son, and her resolve collapsed.

"Maybe later," she conceded. "For now, we need to get your sister down for her nap." The baby had fallen into a loose-limbed sleep on the ride home. "Then I could use your help in the café."

"But, Mo-om—"

Courtney cut him off. "You got into a fight at school today, Josh," she reminded him quietly. "There are consequences for your behavior."

Silence filled the car while her son averted his eyes and stared belligerently out the window. Though his jaw was clenched, Courtney noted the sheen of angry tears. She exhaled. Somewhere beneath that glowering exterior existed the soft-hearted boy who used to climb onto her lap for bedtime stories.

Would she ever see that child again?

She'd scoured the parenting books looking for answers. They all said basically the same thing—that one day, tempered by all he'd been through, Josh would outgrow this phase. It would just take time. Time and love and patience.

The last two she had in spades. As for the other, thanks to this most recent dustup, it sounded as if she and Josh would be spending plenty of quality time together. She crossed her fingers and hoped the experts were right.

"You can wait for me in your room," she said at last. "I'll come see you as soon as I finish with Addie."

On her way up the stairs to the back entrance of their apartment, she considered the best way to get through to the boy. She doubted another long talk would do any good. She'd lectured until they were both tired of hearing her voice, and it hadn't changed a thing.

For the millionth time, she wished she had someone to share the burden—and the joys—of raising her two children. It was the one thing she missed the most about the early days with Ryan, but once baseball had made him famous, he'd treated his family more like a burden than a blessing. She shook her head. Dwelling on the past wasn't going to solve her immediate problems.

At the top of the wooden staircase she flinched when the door to Josh's room slammed shut. Still, Addie stirred only briefly as Courtney settled the little one in her crib. Dreading the heart-to-heart chat that was next on her agenda, she knocked on her son's door and, exercising a parent's prerogative, stepped inside without waiting for an invitation. She ignored the posters of superheroes that dominated the walls, her focus drawn to the small figure huddled on the bed.

She stiffened her spine. "So what happened at school today? Why were you and the other boy fighting?"

For one long heartbeat, she was afraid Josh wouldn't answer, wouldn't turn to face her. At last, with a noisy exhale, he rolled over onto his back. He stared up at the sloping ceiling for a long minute.

"Dylan and some guys were arguing," he finally said, his voice taut. "Dylan said Manny Ramirez was the best player who ever lived. One of the other guys said Dad was. Then Dylan laughed and said Ryan Smith was a washed-up has-been."

Since Ryan's death, Josh so rarely spoke of his father that getting into a fight over him surprised her. Looking into her son's pain-filled eyes, she searched for the right words.

"I know that must have hurt. It hurts me when people say things like that about your dad."

"Dad was a jerk, but I couldn't let Dylan get away with that stuff." As if daring her to contradict the truth, Josh folded his arms across his chest. "So...so I...I pushed him. And he...he pushed me back. Then Mr. Oak was there. He wanted us to shake hands and be friends, but Dylan, he said..." Josh shoved himself into a sitting position.

"What'd he say?" A long list of accusations had been hurled against her late husband. Most of them were true. Afraid Dylan might have chosen one of the juicier tidbits, she held her breath.

Her little boy's chin wobbled. "He called Dad the biggest joke in baseball. He said the Twisters were better off without him."

Courtney swallowed. She studied the tiny face where a smattering of freckles dotted smooth skin beneath eyes that looked too old for their years. She suspected Josh knew far more about the circumstances surrounding his father's death than any ten-year-old should, but apparently, Dylan hadn't. Relieved she wouldn't have to have *that* talk with her young son, she patted his arm.

"And that's when you punched him?"

"Yeah. Dylan swung at me, too, but I was the one who had to go to Principal Morgan's office. He only had to see the nurse. That's not right. He started it. He shoulda gotten in trouble."

She gave his arm a squeeze. "Principal Morgan will take care of Dylan. I want to talk about you. You know it was wrong to push him. And worse to hit him. You should have walked away."

Josh's chin jutted out. "Dad got mad. Plenty of times. He argued with the umpires. He was in fights."

"Yes, but what you don't know is that he paid for those fights." Courtney winced, remembering the last time Ryan had charged the mound after a wild pitch brushed his shoulder. If she had to name the one incident that had started the downward slide for baseball's legendary hitter, she'd point to the bench-clearing brawl that followed. "Every single time he got tossed out of a game or argued with the umpire, he had to pay a big fine."

"Really, Mom?" Josh's eyes widened slightly.

"Really." She took a deep breath. "Now, you have to pay for your mistake. You've been suspended from school. You might be expelled." She watched her son's brow wrinkle. "Do you know what that means?"

Josh plucked at the covers on his bed. "Not exactly."

"Principal Morgan said you can't go back to Orange Blossom. Because you broke a very important rule, he says you might have to transfer to the Alternative Center."

The creases on Josh's face told her that even her son had heard of the special school.

"But that's where they send the really mean kids!" he protested.

"And you're too good to go there," she assured him. "Instead, I'll be your teacher for now. We'll set up a desk for you here in your room where you can do your lessons."

"No school?" Josh's eyes widened. His mouth dropped open.

Courtney maintained her matter-of-fact expression despite her roiling insides. She'd appeal the principal's decision, of course, but until someone higher up the chain overruled him, homeschooling her son was the best option.

Josh stared at the four colorful walls as if he were looking at a prison cell. "That's not fair!" he shouted. "I hate it here! I hate you for making us come here." He wrenched his pillow from the bed and threw it across the room. "I miss my toys. And my friends. And my old school. Why'd you make us leave?"

The angry outburst struck Courtney straight in the stomach. Even though she knew he didn't mean what he was saying, that he was simply giving in to the heat of the moment, it took every ounce of her control not to double over.

Buying them both a much-needed minute, she stood. Her heart felt as if it weighed a ton as she crossed to the door and closed it. Every tear that streamed down her son's beet-red cheeks tightened her chest when she returned to his side. She placed a trembling hand on the boy's leg. "No matter what you say, Josh, I love you."

He swiped at his face. His voice strangled by angry tears, he demanded, "Why, Mom? Why'd you make us come here?"

She didn't want to heap more blame on his dad—the press had done a good enough job of that. But it was past time her child learned that sometimes even adults had to make tough choices. She struggled for an answer a ten-year-old could both understand and accept.

"A big house like our old one is expensive," she said, as simply as possible. "Without the big paycheck your dad made playing baseball, we didn't have enough money to live there anymore. This little apartment and the café downstairs—it's all we can afford."

Josh's mouth gaped wider. "We can't *ever* go back to our old house?"

"Is that what you thought, honey? That one day we'd move back there?"

His head bobbed.

A lot of her son's anger and frustration over the past few months made more sense if he'd been biding his time, waiting for things to return to normal. More than anything, she wanted him to understand, to start accepting their new life. Whether they liked it or not, this *was* their new normal.

"You and your sister are the most important things in the world to me, Josh. I want you to be happy. Now that you know we can't ever move back to Orlando, do you think you can work with me here? Try a little harder to be a good boy?"

For a second, she thought she'd gotten through to him. She watched him study the room the way he might if he were seeing it the first time.

"Mom," he said after a long pause. "Mom, I can't get homeschooled. There's no place to put a desk." He pointed to the furniture that crowded the walls. "Can't you tell Principal Morgan I'm sorry? I'll…" He took a quivering breath. "I'll tell Dylan I'm sorry. And Mr. Oak, too."

The boy had a point. Though she'd taken pains to turn

the small room under the eaves into a homey, welcoming space, there was hardly enough room for his bed, dresser and bookcase. Downstairs wouldn't work, either. It was bad enough that she divided her time between Addie and her customers. Adding an active ten-year-old into the mix would spell disaster for her struggling business. Besides, Josh needed to be around kids his own age.

Her heart sank. She could give him what he needed. But it would mean doing the one thing she'd sworn she'd never do again.

One season, she told herself. One season.

She gritted her teeth and offered, "There is another choice. Principal Morgan said if you played Little League for Coach Oak, he'd let you come back to school on Monday."

Hope brightened Josh's eyes. "Please, Mom," he begged. "I'll do better at school."

"You'll study hard? You know your grades need to come up."

"Yes, Mom. Anything. I'll do anything."

"Anything?" She grinned and poked him in the ribs. "I need to go downstairs and clean up the mess I left there this morning. You—" she pushed Josh's hair out of his eyes "—you need to clean up this room." She gave the pile of dirty clothes on the floor a meaningful glance.

Josh scrambled off his bed. By the time she made it to the door, he'd scooped up the first few items. He looked around the room as if he had no idea where to put them.

"In the hamper?" she suggested. She shook her head and wondered if ignoring the laundry basket was somehow embedded in the male genetic code.

As first steps went, Josh's cooperation wasn't much, but thankful for even the smallest change in his attitude, she headed downstairs. In the café's open kitchen, she quickly swept the spoiled salad ingredients into the trash and ran the soup through the garbage disposal. While she worked, she fretted.

Could she really let Josh play Little League?

It went against everything she wanted for him. Every baseball player she knew was egotistical, self-centered, cocky. They lived, breathed and dreamed the sport. She knew firsthand they didn't start out that way. Yes, Ryan had been serious about making it into the pros, but he'd changed after he'd made it big. Baseball had changed him.

Would it change Josh?

A lot would depend on his coach. The man would have a huge influence over her son. Quickly she reviewed the little she knew about Travis Oak. Tall, ruggedly handsome, sure of himself. But his willingness to sacrifice winning by putting Josh on his team didn't quite fit the big-league player mold. Still, that didn't mean she trusted him.

At the first sign that baseball was having a negative impact on Josh, she'd yank him off Travis's team. Of course, to do her duty as a parent, she'd have to watch the coach very carefully. And if she happened to enjoy the view, what was the harm?

Chapter Three

Saturday morning Travis rounded third and headed for home while chalk spilled, thick and straight, from the cart he pushed along the base path of Field Number One. Across the diamond a dad anchored second base into place. More fathers hauled long tables from the rec center to a tent where volunteers would pin numbers on T-shirts and check names off lists. Returning players, on the lookout for broken bottles or other dangerous objects, walked shoulder to shoulder across the freshly mowed outfield as coaches and parents wrapped up preparations for tryouts.

Finished with the line marker, Travis slapped his hands together. The move created a cloud of white dust that mingled with the odor of hot dogs and popcorn from the snack bar. Though he'd never admit it, the smell was one of the things he loved best about baseball.

As the first of several minivans pulled off Barton Boulevard into McLarty Park, he staked out a good vantage point. Searching for likely candidates to fill the open spots on his team roster, Travis swept over novices who didn't know better than to show up in shorts and tennis shoes. Instead, he focused on kids in baseball pants worn at the knees, cleats that had seen a season or two of use. A tiny little princess in a tutu marched past carrying a bat far longer than she was. He gave the girl a wide grin before making note of a dozen more-likely candidates to watch.

But did he need three new players? Or four?

The answer depended on whether or not Josh Smith showed up, and Travis scanned the families milling about the parking lot.

No pretty baby-toting woman with a lanky young boy in sight.

He'd almost given up hope when he spotted Courtney beside an aging sedan. The objects she pulled from the trunk of her car dashed cold water on a budding fantasy, but the stroller and assorted items that soon littered the ground at her feet seemed like a lot for her slight figure. Never one to be remiss in his manners, Travis wandered over to lend a hand.

On his way, he couldn't help but run through a few opening lines. Nothing seemed good enough. He was working on some new material when he spotted Josh climbing out of the Smiths' backseat. Travis groaned. Making a pass at a widow in front of her ready-made family was such a bad idea he shoved it aside.

"Hey, Josh," he said, focusing on the child. He gave the kid's baggy shorts and tennis shoes a once over. Okay, so the youngster was going to need a *lot* of help. "You ready for tryouts?"

While Courtney rounded the car to stand beside her son, Josh smacked his fist into an adult-sized fielder's glove. "There's a lot of kids here, Coach Oak. Does everyone get to play?" Staring at all the activity, he looked like a child who'd never stepped onto a Little League field before.

Which he hadn't, Travis reminded himself.

"Yep. Today we'll separate all these boys and girls into two divisions—majors and minors. In the minors, younger players learn and get the experience they need to make it to the next level. Older kids and ones with better skills play in the majors. I coach the Sluggers," he said, pointing to his bright green jersey. "We're in the majors."

For a kid who'd never swung a bat outside of P.E., Josh was sharp enough to know the score. Doubt colored his little face. "I might not be good enough to make your team."

Travis caught the same uncertainty in Courtney's expression.

"Don't worry," he said as much for her benefit as the boy's. "We'll practice for a month before our first game."

He averted his eyes and fought the urge to whistle "Dixie" while Courtney stretched into the backseat to retrieve her daughter.

How was a man not supposed to gape at slender thighs and well-turned calves?

The answer emerged from the car propped on Courtney's slim hip. She blotted a bit of drool from her daughter's chin, then tilted her head to look into his face. "So what's the, um, game plan?"

For a moment, Travis got lost in the light dusting of freckles across Courtney's upturned nose, the slight pout of pink lips. Something in his chest shifted, and he started, suddenly aware that he'd been staring. He quickly explained the sign-in process. Then, eager to move on, he started to say he'd see her later.

A single glance at Josh stopped him. The boy stared at the fields where fathers and their sons tossed warm-up pitches to one another, and Travis's throat constricted.

He gave himself a mental kick in the pants. What had he been thinking? He couldn't leave an inexperienced child to fend for himself.

He rolled the shoulder of his pitching arm. "In the rush to get things ready this morning, I haven't had a chance to warm up." With a pointed glance toward her son, he turned to Courtney. "Think you and Addie can get him signed in while Josh and I throw the ball around?"

"I think we could do that. If it's okay with Josh." Courtney's gaze swung to the youngster, whose longing was too poignant to ignore.

"Yeah." The boy sucked in a breath that was half relief, half eager yearning. "Yeah, Mom."

When the tiniest smile tugged at the corners of the young mother's lips, Travis slapped a hand on the boy's shoulder. He gave Josh a grin and aimed a wider one at Courtney before he steered them to a patch of grass none of the other players had claimed. Telling himself he was only making sure she knew the way, he spared a quick glance in Courtney's direction.

"Ready, Coach," Josh called.

Travis gave himself a shake.

"Let's start by letting me see how well you can catch." Mentally, he crossed his fingers, hoping the kid at least knew the rudiments.

Josh sank into an effortless crouch, his knees bent, his feet planted shoulder width apart. Except for the huge glove, the kid looked like a major leaguer, but Travis tossed him a slow grounder. The boy scooped it up and fired it back at him as if he'd been playing shortstop all his life.

"This isn't your first time doing this," Travis observed when the ball smacked into his glove harder than he'd expected. Slipping the leather off his hand, he gave his fingers an exaggerated shake to let the boy know he'd thrown some heat. He pitched again, this time putting a little more zing on the ball, and watched the kid field it easily. "Your dad teach you how to throw?"

"Nah. Mr. David and me, we used to play catch at our old house."

The ball arced perfectly into Travis's glove, bringing a little twinge of jealousy along with it. Hating himself for asking, he chucked another question with the next grounder. "So does Mr. David come see you now that you've moved here?"

"Uh-uh. He worked for my dad. And he's—" Josh's face scrunched "—gone."

Sorry he'd asked, Travis framed the next pitch. *Pop.* The ball slapped into his glove. He returned the throw, this time a little harder, and shook his head in wonder when Josh tracked the speed and moved to intercept it.

"Good job," he told the boy.

For the next few minutes, he put the youngster through his usual warm-ups. Josh never missed. In fact, he did so well Travis began to think he'd gotten the better end of the bargain he'd made with Bob Morgan. Motioning the boy to him, he folded the ball into his glove and shoved it under his arm, smiling.

"You looked good out there." Though Courtney had no reason to lie about it, he asked, "You sure you haven't played before? Not T-ball? Maybe Pony League?"

"No, Coach." The child stopped to readjust the floppy glove he'd tucked under his arm the same way Travis had. "I went with my mom to watch the Orlando Twisters play. But I've never been on a field like this one." The youngster looked around. "It's smaller, but it's kind of nice."

Josh's face was so open and honest Travis had to believe him. Convinced he'd stumbled on a natural-born fielder, he itched to find out if the kid could swing a bat. Before they could move to the cages, though, music blared from the announcer's booth.

"That means tryouts are getting ready to start," he told Josh. "I have to help the other coaches get things organized, so I need you to run on up to your mom and have her pin your number on the back of your shirt. She'll tell you where to go next. You got that?"

For the first time since they'd started tossing the ball around, Josh looked uncertain.

Travis reached deep, dredging up the memory of his own first tryout. He'd been a lot younger than the boy in front of him, but he remembered feeling scared and thrilled all at the same time. He tried to recall what his dad had said to him on that occasion and came up empty.

"I…uh…I…" he started. He stared down into a face that had gone two shades lighter. Seeing the kid's nervousness, he drew in a steadying breath. "Look, I know you might not do as well as some of the other boys out here today, but everybody needs to learn new stuff. Even them. You just do your best and try to have a good time."

As speeches went, it wasn't *his* best, but watching the color flood back into Josh's face ignited a warm feeling in Travis's chest.

"You got nothing to worry about, kid."

He centered Josh's baseball cap over the boy's hair and pointed him toward the shade trees. It wasn't until he raised a hand to signal Courtney that he realized she'd been watching them the whole time. She sprang to her feet, a wide smile breaking across her face. For a second, her pleased expression made his pulse race. Then Josh cut between them. By the time he could see her again, Courtney was on her knees hugging her son.

What had he been thinking?

Courtney Smith had no more interest in him than he had in a woman who didn't like sports. Sure, she was cute and possessed an amazing pair of legs. But he'd set his sights on coaching pro ball. And lately his old team, the Norfolk Cannons, had shown a lot of interest. Once their call came—probably by the end of the summer—he'd be on the road again. Which made another in a long list of reasons why he should stay as far away from Courtney as possible.

His lecture finished, he blew a calming breath over his lips. Baseball. He was here to play baseball. Not to watch women who were all wrong for him. An entire Little League season loomed ahead. If he was going to have a decent team, he had to concentrate on the kids he'd pick in tonight's draft.

Throughout the rest of the day, Travis worked hard to keep his focus where it belonged. He noted the names and numbers of a dozen good solid players. He spoke to their parents, made decisions about which ones he'd choose if he got the chance. Through it all, he allowed himself only the occasional glimpse of the woman who sat among the other parents beneath the trees. Almost every time he stole a look, her eyes were tracking her son's movements, but there were a couple of times he swore she was watching him, too.

Once, he caught her smiling, though he almost preferred the pensive frown she usually aimed in his direction. It told him she hadn't quite made up her mind about him, and that suited him just fine. Even a confirmed bachelor like he was had to admit that Addie, with her drooly chin and big blue eyes so much like her mom's, was kind of cute, but a ready-made family didn't fit his plans for the future.

As for Josh, the more he saw of the kid, the more confused Travis grew. The boy had a head for the game, that was certain. When the other coaches threw routine grounders at him, Josh knew where the ball would be and got there in time to field it. He caught pop flies as well as many of the kids and better than some. By the time Josh walked to the batter's box, Travis was scratching his head and wondering how a kid who'd never stepped onto a ball field before had drawn the attention of every coach in the league. They lined the fences when Josh stepped to the plate.

Travis held his breath. The first pitch was low and outside. A murmur of surprise rippled through the coaching staff when Josh's bat sliced through empty air. The youngster shook his head and squared up for the next one. This time he managed to connect, though Travis was pretty sure the hit was pure dumb luck. The kid's eyes were closed when his bat met the ball.

One by one, the rest of the coaches lost interest and drifted off as Josh missed easy throws and swung at bad ones. Spectators and parents still crowded the bleachers, though. One of them jeered when the boy swung at a pitch so far over his head he'd have needed a ladder to actually make contact.

Immediately, anger flooded Josh's face. The boy slung his bat and stalked off the field.

Shooting the offender in the stands a dark look, Travis hurried after the kid. He caught up with Josh on the far side of the dugout. The boy's shoulders slumped. Furious tears streaked his face. He pressed his back against the concrete wall.

Travis leaned down, his head buzzing. He'd dealt with angry young boys and a few out-of-control parents in his time. Every coach did. But for reasons he didn't quite understand, getting the point across to this one was more important than it had ever been.

"Hey, you did a great job out there," he began. "In fact, you did so well that I'm going to let you in on a little secret. I'm glad you didn't get a lot of hits today."

Josh's head snapped up. "That's a lie," he spit. "You need good hitters on your team. I can't hit."

The kid reminded him so much of himself that Travis's heart nearly melted. "Nope, it's true," he said, giving the boy an indifferent shrug. "In fact, I was hoping you wouldn't shine much at all."

Josh swiped the tail of his T-shirt over his face. "That's crazy talk," he sniffed, but he didn't look away.

"No, it's coach talk," Travis corrected. "You made my job a lot easier when you missed that last pitch. I won't have to worry about some other coach snapping you up before I have a chance to draft you to the Sluggers tonight. I want you on my team, Josh."

Travis straightened. That he was telling the unvarnished truth came as a big surprise.

Conflicting emotions played across Josh's face. "Really?" he asked.

"Really," Travis assured him. He waited until he was certain the boy believed him. "I have some ideas about what we can do to help you hit better. We'll talk about that later. For now, though, no more throwing the bat around, okay?"

Josh toed one tennis shoe through the grass before he met Travis's gaze. "Sorry, Coach," he said. "I won't."

Travis didn't fool himself. The kid had issues, and it'd take more than one off-the-cuff talk to resolve them. But for now, an apology and a promise were good enough. He swatted the brim of the boy's baseball hat and told him to join the rest of his group for the pitching tryouts that would wrap up the day.

Turning, he decided he'd done a good enough job with her son that he'd earned himself another glimpse of Courtney. Only he didn't expect to spot her standing at the end of the dugout, her hands on her slim hips. Travis whistled. If looks could kill, the woman would make a world-class assassin.

Worse—he gulped—she stared straight at him.

HAVING RACED TO the field, Courtney swung toward the coach, prepared to give the man a piece of her mind for letting Josh get away with such outrageous behavior. She'd seen the harm anger caused when it was unleashed on the ball field. People got hurt. Careers were ended. Lives were irrevocably changed. Travis might think he had a plan for dealing with Josh's emotional outbursts, but he'd obviously never considered the danger of putting a virtual club in an angry boy's hands.

What if Principal Morgan found out? Deal or no deal, he'd carry through on his decision to expel Josh.

And then what would become of her son?

Telling herself she had to be the strong one, had to end this now before something worse happened, she stood, her feet rooted in gravel and red dirt.

One look at Travis's confident smile, and her resolve wavered.

"Hey," he said softly. "Where'd you come from? Where's Addie?" He studied her as if he expected the baby to materialize in her arms.

"Melinda Markham has her." She gestured toward the trees where, until moments ago, she'd taken advantage of the opportunity to make friends with a few of the other moms. "I rushed over here to take Josh home, but…" Tears clogged her throat. "Did I hear right? You still want him on your team?"

Travis's searching gaze roamed her face. Questions formed on his handsome features. "Why wouldn't I? Nothing's changed."

"But he…he lost his temper," she protested. Whenever a professional ballplayer did something like that, he faced stiff penalties.

"No harm. No foul." The big man shrugged. "He learned something. Next time, he'll think about it before he lets one bad appearance at the plate get to him."

Travis's reaction was so different from what she'd expected that she gaped at him.

"I know you're worried about him, but trust me. He's not the worst kid I've dealt with. He'll come around."

Relief at finding someone who shared her opinion of Josh triggered tears she'd held at bay for far too long. As they rolled unchecked down her cheeks, she never saw Travis move. One second he was standing at the opposite end of the dugout. The next he was simply in front of her, shielding her from prying eyes. He stood so close she caught a whiff of his aftershave mingled with the faint musky scent of a man who'd spent the better part of the day in the sun. His large hands cupped her elbows, and she gasped.

Heat shot from his fingertips and spread up her arms.

Her head came up and she met his deep brown eyes. What she saw there spread a delicious feeling right through her midsection.

"Look, all kids get upset from time to time. Learning how to control their temper and frustration, that's just part of the game."

The game. The baseball *game.*

Courtney's heart stuttered. The tingly sparks ignited by Travis's touch died. A vague hunger faded. She crossed her arms over her chest and stepped back, letting cold air fill the space between them. Travis wasn't interested in her. She was a fool to think he might be. No man, no single man, would want any part of her baggage. Or her secrets.

"I'd better get back to Addie, then. I'll…uh…I'll talk to you later."

Making a dignified escape was difficult considering the way her legs protested each step she took away from Travis. Unable to help herself, she snagged a final look over her shoulder. The coach stood where she'd left him, a bemused expression on his face.

And no wonder. Her emotions were all over the map. He probably thought she was nuts. Which was really a shame. Big, strong, impressive Travis had arms a girl could get lost in. For a moment there, she'd wanted to bury herself in his wide chest. Wanted more than that, if she were brutally honest about it.

She nearly tripped over the idea.

Not that she'd ever consider a fling, she corrected. She knew herself too well. A casual affair was so far beyond her comfort zone it was laughable. Besides, there was the little matter of interest—and Travis was more focused on helping her son than on her. Which was what she wanted, right?

Exactly!

She drew in a breath filled with resolve. Steeling herself against the feelings Travis had stirred, she returned to her place with the rest of the moms.

"You *bolted* out of here so fast Addie didn't even *miss* you." Tommy's mom, Melinda Markham, could make anything sound dramatic. "Is Josh *okay?*"

"He's fine," Courtney answered as smoothly as her racing heart would allow. "Travis talked to him."

"He brings out the *best* in the boys. This will be Tommy's third year on his team, and I've never heard Coach raise his voice." Melinda leaned close enough to whisper. "If it weren't for my Tom, that man could leave his cleats under my bed anytime."

At her friend's wicked grin, a laugh bubbled up from Courtney's center.

"He's really not my type," she whispered in return. She gave herself a pat on the back for managing to sound disinterested, though it was harder than she imagined to remember why no baseball player ever would be.

The group beneath the trees thinned as families departed after their youngsters' pitching tryouts. When the coaches handed Josh the ball, Courtney gave her son a good hard look. The boy had his father's long lean frame. His talent, too, if she was any judge. Having spent a good part of her life around baseball players, she thought she might be.

Had he also inherited Ryan's foul temper, his philandering ways?

She pushed her fears aside as Josh went into his windup. His throws were erratic, no doubt, but he threw the ball hard. With practice and the right kind of coaching, she knew he could bring it into the strike zone.

And then what?

"Mom, did you see me? Coach Oak says I did real good." Hero worship glowed in her son's eyes a few minutes after tryouts ended.

"That's right." Travis clapped the boy on the back. Pride danced in the gaze he gave Josh. "You'll do even better next time. And the time after that." He practically beamed at Courtney. "I think your son has the makings of a great ballplayer."

A bright smile firmly in place for her son's sake, Courtney stifled a groan. Travis's assessment was exactly what she didn't want to hear.

One season. In exchange for keeping him in school, she'd promised to let Josh play one season of Little League. Not even the best coach could hone his natural talent in just a few months, could he?

Something inside her warned that if anyone could, it'd be Travis Oak.

She scanned his face, hoping he was simply blowing the kind of smoke all coaches fed their players. No such luck. From the way he looked at Josh, he was already envisioning the boy's future in the major leagues.

Which wasn't going to happen. Not if she had anything to do with it.

"I have one condition," she said in a firm voice. She braced for the argument that was sure to erupt. "I'll let Josh play for the Sluggers, but only if I can attend every practice, watch every game." At the first sign that Travis had anything more than one Little League season in mind for her boy, she'd yank her son off his team. Agreement or no agreement.

Travis's easy smile caught her off guard. "Well, that's great!" he exclaimed. "I've been looking for a new team mom. Since you'll be there anyway, you might as well take the job."

Too late, Courtney sensed a trap. "What would I have to do?"

Looking far too pleased, Travis scuffed a foot through the grass. "Oh, you know," he hedged. "Help out with schedules and snacks. Pull together the team roster. Organize team pictures. There's more, but you and I can go over all the details when we meet."

"It sounds as if we'd need to work pretty closely together." Behind her sunglasses, she let her eyes narrow. Keeping an eye on Travis at the ball field was one thing. Could she keep her distance if she had to work with him several times a week?

"That's not a problem, is it?" He removed his hat, ran a hand through thick hair.

Aware that Josh stood nearby, she couldn't very well admit why it was. Her mouth went so dry her "No" was barely audible.

"Good," Travis said, snugging his hat back on. "So how 'bout tomorrow afternoon?"

She started to object, but the coach was one step ahead of her. "Don't worry about Josh and Addie." He shrugged. "I spend my entire day around kids." He squatted at the edge of the blanket. "And aren't you a cutie," he said, chucking the baby's wet chin.

Instantly entranced, her traitorous daughter held out chubby arms and waited to be held. Travis beamed a smile but stood. "I'd better not," he said, pointing to his jersey. "I'd get her all dirty. So tomorrow?"

She swallowed. "Addie takes a nap around two. Swing by then. We can meet downstairs in the café."

"Two it is. I'd better get back," he said, gesturing at the coaches and volunteers who were storing gear and dismantling the sign-in tent. He turned to Josh. "I'll talk to you later. After the draft."

Watching Travis's long strides take him back to the field, Courtney feared she'd just made the biggest mistake of her life. Not only had she agreed to let her son participate in the sport that had left her alone to raise her children, but she'd signed up to spend time with a man who disturbed her equilibrium far more than he should. The only solution was to keep him at arm's length. She held out her hands and groaned.

Her arms weren't long enough for such an impossible task.

Chapter Four

Strategically placed stop signs and narrow lanes slowed traffic through Cocoa Village, where colorful window displays and shaded benches tempted visitors to linger. Travis braked to let a vehicle pull out of a spot four doors down from Coffee on Brevard. He maneuvered his Jeep into the parallel parking space and grabbed the overflowing shoebox from the seat beside him.

With any luck, he'd hand the team-mom duties off to Courtney in a matter of minutes, leaving all afternoon to work out an unaccustomed restlessness in the batting cages. He leaned into his seat. Much as he didn't want to admit it, he'd been unsettled ever since the day Josh's mom walked into Principal Morgan's office.

Why did she get under his skin?

He shrugged the thought aside. It didn't matter. Slowly, he shook his head and stepped from the car, determined to keep his focus from straying where it didn't belong.

On the sidewalk, he inhaled a gulp of cool winter air that tasted of salt from the nearby river.

"Yo, Travis! Good to see you, man. You think Lester's arm will get the Cannons through the play-offs this year?"

Travis pivoted toward the corner where a wizened

figure hawked magazines and papers from behind a plywood stand.

"Afternoon, Manny," he said, nodding. "Norfolk's playing strong. As for Lester, ask me again in October."

Manny's grin deepened. "You woulda taken them all the way, Travis. Remember that shutout you pitched against the—" Manny stopped to tug on his hat brim. "Who was it, the Biloxi Tides or the Columbia Pines?"

Both, actually, though Travis wouldn't admit to it. "Sorry." He dropped a dollar on the closest magazine stack. "Gotta run. I have an appointment with the Sluggers' new team mom." He hooked a thumb over his shoulder at the coffee shop down the street. "I'm already late." The phone calls to the new players on his team had taken a bigger bite out of his day than he'd anticipated.

"Ms. Smith?" Manny slipped the money into the oilskin apron that hung from his slim hips. He squinted at a window where Coffee on Brevard had been elaborately etched into the plate glass. "She's a quiet one. Every once in a while, she sends me a cuppa coffee. Pretty good, that."

"If you say so, I'll be sure to check it out. Catch ya later, Manny."

Beneath the café's jaunty awning, Travis stepped past tiny wrought-iron tables and delicate chairs to hold the door for two departing customers. The stylishly dressed women stopped their chatter as they passed. He tipped his head, returning their appraising glances with his usual polite, if practiced, smile.

He stepped across the threshold into a room where coffee-scented air reminded him of his childhood home. Sturdy tables scattered about the main dining area made even a man his size comfortable.

"Can I help you?"

Travis swung toward the counter, where a teenager in a dark green apron was giving him the once-over.

"Nicole," he said with a quick glance at her name tag. "Is Ms. Smith around? She said to meet her here."

While the girl's initial greeting lost some of its wattage, a chair scraped the floor in the back of the room. "Hey, Coach Oak," came a familiar voice.

Travis followed the sound to a spot where school books littered a table. "Josh, hi. I'm supposed to drop this stuff off with your mom."

Blue eyes much like Courtney's tracked the cardboard box that Travis shifted from one hand to another. "I'll… uh…I'll get her," Josh offered. He raced for the stairs but stopped when he reached them. His hand on the banister, one foot poised over the first step, he turned a hope-filled face toward Travis. "Um, Coach?"

"Yeah?"

"Thanks for putting me on your team."

"No problem, kid." Travis tossed the boy a smile. "Our first practice is Tuesday at five. Get there a half hour early and we'll work on your hitting."

Josh's face brightened. "Sure thing, Coach." He raced up the steps.

Travis ordered a cup of coffee and made himself at home at one of the tables. Five minutes passed before a squeak at the top of the stairs caught his attention. He marshaled an oh-so-casual smile that took more effort than he expected to keep steady once Courtney stepped onto the landing.

He'd have sworn they'd shared a link, a spark, a connection behind the dugout. But judging from her appearance, the attraction was all one-sided. His. He took a breath. Not that he considered himself a *catch* or anything, but women usually put some effort into earning his attention.

Not Courtney.

From a careless ponytail to a blousy shirt and loose-fitting pants that didn't do justice to her curvy figure, not one thing about the fresh-faced blonde acknowledged their moment at the ball field. But if she'd meant to disguise her assets, her plan had backfired. The disheveled look only made her appear impossibly small and vulnerable.

He fought an insistent urge to rush up the stairs and sling a protective arm around her shoulders. Knowing she didn't need his help and probably wouldn't appreciate it, he gripped the edge of the table instead. He held on until her feet struck the hardwood floor. Then, and only then, he stood.

"Courtney, good to see you," he said, trying not to second-guess his every move. Meanwhile, Josh tripped down the stairs behind his mom. The boy skidded across the floor in a very baseball-like slide that ended at his own table.

"Travis."

The small hand Courtney slipped into his sent a brain-numbing tingle straight up his arm. He scoured her face, certain this time he'd find the same surprised reaction to his touch mirrored in her features. Disappointment struck when she dropped his hand as if it stung. Her face hidden, she turned toward the girl behind the counter.

"Nicole," Courtney called. "Are there any of those almond croissants left?"

"We're all out," the teen chirped. "We still have some cookies, though."

"Good. Bring those and— Do you want another cup of coffee, Travis?"

Though she tried hard to disguise it, he caught a tempting shimmer in the blue eyes that met his own. His gut tightened, a reaction he insisted was due entirely to the fact that he'd skipped lunch. It had nothing to do with Courtney, he swore. Nothing at all.

"No more coffee," he said, "but I could handle a few cookies."

Munching on them sounded like a good distraction. Of course, taking the treats *to go* was an even better idea. Aware that Josh was watching, he swept the box he'd toted into the café from the table.

"Here," he said, thrusting it toward her.

Courtney glanced down, her brow furrowing. "What's all this?" She poked gingerly beneath the top sheets.

Travis showed her his palms. "It's everything Marty's mom gave me at the end of the season."

To tell the truth, he had no idea what the box contained. Three sons had provided his previous team mom with enough experience that she handled the duties with little input from him. He'd expected Courtney to do likewise. But one look at the questions that played across her face and he knew, no matter what he'd expected, he wasn't going to get it.

Thumbing through the papers, she sank onto a chair. "We need to get organized."

Travis caught her note of dismay. Mentally, he calculated the time it'd take to fill her in on all the activities the league had planned. By the time they finished, it'd be too late to hit the batting cages. He guessed he'd have to get used to feeling tense whenever he was around a certain off-limits blonde.

"Okay," he agreed. "But I don't work for free." He chose a nut-studded cookie from the platter Nicole had placed between them. Attributing the contentment that washed through him to what tasted like equal parts butter and sugar, he slid into the chair next to Courtney's. Soon piles of paper and instructions littered the table, along with more than a few crumbs.

"Three o'clock, Ms. Smith," Nicole announced after they'd worked steadily for an hour.

Courtney pushed away from the table, the call tree they'd created dropping from her fingers. "Time to close up shop."

Travis checked his watch. "Early, isn't it?"

"I open at seven to catch people on their way to work, but business usually dies out by midafternoon. Not much call for caffeine this late in the day," she said with a grin.

Travis let the breath he'd been holding escape as she rose and crossed to the front doors. He steeled himself against the fragrance of shampoo that tickled his nose and drove him to distraction. While Courtney keyed the dead bolt behind Nicole and flipped the Open sign to Closed, he shook the strain from fingers that seemed intent on finding an excuse to brush against one of Courtney's smooth arms or the back of one of her delicate hands.

Turning, she caught him in midstretch. "Had enough for one day?"

Travis flexed his fingers a final time before he put them to work straightening the edges of one of the neat piles she'd erected from his jumbled mess. "No. I'm good. Let's finish." The sooner he wrapped things up here, the sooner he could hit the gym, go for a run, anything to burn off his tension.

"We'll have to stop when Addie gets up from her nap." Courtney canted her head toward the baby monitor on a nearby table. "Let's see…. Every parent needs to work in the concession and send snacks twice. Is that about it?"

Travis eyed her checklist. She was both right and wrong. There were other issues they hadn't tackled. Items that hadn't made it to her list yet. "Well, we only need the treats for practices. The league provides snow cones for the entire team after every game."

"Great." She adjusted the schedule. "I'll call every-one tonight and—"

Babbling sounds kept her from completing the sen-tence. She turned to the boy who'd labored over his homework with barely a grumble. "Could you check on your sister while Coach Oak and I finish up?"

Courtney's pert features swung back to him. "We're almost done here, aren't we?"

"Yeah," he agreed, torn between springing to his feet and staying put long enough to ask questions he didn't want Josh to overhear.

"Can we go to the park later, Mom?" the boy asked as he crossed the room.

"Have you finished all your assignments?" Courtney countered. "I want you to be all caught up when you go back to school tomorrow."

"I left my papers out so you can check them," he said, rushing up the stairs.

"Great. His homework is my homework." She sighed.

"It never ends, does it?" Travis asked, not bothering to hide his respect for anyone who could juggle a new business with the monumental task of raising two kids.

"Not really." Courtney sipped coffee that had to be ice-cold.

More aware than he wanted to be that Josh's departure left them alone for the first time that day, Travis pondered what to do next. Making a fast exit was the smart move. But there was still the little matter of her son. Josh might just be the most talented kid Travis had ever seen. Trouble was, the boy needed to look the part. Right now, he didn't.

He took a breath. "Josh'll need baseball pants and cleats for our first practice."

Courtney's pencil stopped moving across the paper. "I thought the league provided uniforms."

"They do." He nodded. "Bats, balls, catcher's gear. Batting helmets, too. But not all the other stuff. Pants with thick pads will keep him from getting scraped up when he slides. Cleats will protect his ankles and give him better traction. To play without them is risky."

Courtney wrote the words on a slip of paper. She underlined each. "How much, do you think?"

"Walmart and Target have 'em. They shouldn't run more than fifty bucks. You can pay more—a lot more—but it's not at all necessary."

He hesitated. If he was reading Courtney right, she didn't have a lot of loose cash floating around. That made his next topic even tougher. He took a sec to remind himself that baseball would solve Josh's problems the same way it had been the answer to his own.

"Now, about his glove." He let his voice drop. "It was his dad's, wasn't it?"

Courtney jerked upright so fast the pencil she'd been holding sailed across the table. "Why do you ask?"

Travis grabbed for the pencil, catching it before it rolled off the edge. Perplexed, he searched her face. Tension etched lines across her fine features, but the worry he saw in her blue eyes sent a ripple of unease through him.

"I'm sorry," he backpedaled. "From his school records, I know Josh lost his dad last year. I didn't mean to pry."

Whatever he'd glimpsed in Courtney's eyes, it evaporated so quickly he asked himself if it had really been there at all.

"It's not something I like to talk about." The breath she exhaled carried a ragged note. "It's been rough."

"I can't imagine how hard this has been on all of you." Courtney looked so forlorn that Travis cupped his fingers over hers.

At his touch she shied away. Leaning into her chair, she folded her arms. "Save your sympathy," she said, her voice soft. "Josh's dad wasn't around much. When he was, let's just say *family* wasn't at the top of his priority list."

Travis knew his expression had hardened, but he was powerless to stop it. The idea that Courtney and her sweet kids had had to settle for second place, or judging from her reaction, even third, made him more than a little sick. He shook his head, trying to get his bearings.

"So if I asked Josh to put that glove on a shelf, it wouldn't be a big problem? It really isn't right for Little League, and it sure doesn't fit his hand."

"Not a problem. He barely knew his dad," she said, her voice cool.

That sick feeling in his stomach deepened. He sure as hell hoped he'd be a good enough husband and father that his wife and kids, when he had them, would hold on to his memory. Once more he fought the urge to wrap his arms around Courtney and hold her until the petite blonde knew what it meant to be cherished.

Focus, he told himself.

Expecting her wholehearted agreement, he was caught off guard when she nibbled on her lower lip the way he'd seen her do before.

"I'm not sure I can afford a new glove. Not right now."

There wasn't much he could do about her past, but this was one hurdle he could clear.

"No problem. I have a couple of spares lying around my apartment. I'll drop one by. He can try it out, see if it fits."

Courtney placed her hands palms down on the table-top. "I wasn't asking for your charity."

"And I wasn't offering it. I just want to give Josh his best chance at doing well. Look," he said, frowning, "there's no sense spending a lot of money on something he might outgrow before the season ends. Let him use one of mine. If he sticks with baseball, you can buy him his own next year."

He watched her struggle with the problem without coming up with a better solution. At last her brow smoothed. If the look she turned on him wasn't filled with simpering thankfulness, Travis decided he was okay with that. It was enough to see the trouble fade from her clear blue eyes and a smile play about her lips.

It was time to go.

If he stayed, he'd be tempted to do something he'd be sure to regret.

He stood. A nonchalant *See you Tuesday* died in his throat. He cleared it and tried again. What came out instead was, "I'll swing by in the morning to go over the rest of the stuff."

Courtney glanced past the empty box to the list she'd insisted on making. "There's more?"

"A few things. Team pictures are in three weeks. Then there's the trip to Twister Stadium at the end of the season. We need to start planning that as soon as possible."

He peered at Courtney and wondered why the color had drained from her face.

UNEASE ROLLED THROUGH Courtney's stomach. Just as she'd begun to see him as more than a gung-ho athlete, Travis had dropped a trip to Twister Stadium into the conversation as if it had no more ramifications than a run to the grocery store.

For him maybe it didn't. For her, well, she'd vowed never to set foot inside the place again. She swiveled toward him. "Trip? What trip?"

She sucked in air while Travis searched her face. When they were seated side by side, the man had towered over her. On his feet, peering down at her through concerned eyes, his very male presence filled the room. The forearm he'd lowered onto the table had stretched like a tree limb to a hand that could easily span her waist. Quickly, she squelched the distinctly feminine sensation that whispered through her in response.

"Are you okay?" he asked.

She straightened. "I'm fine." Or she would be once she stuffed her emotions back in the trunk where she'd kept them hidden ever since the day she found out she'd spent too many years with the most unfaithful man on the planet.

She swallowed, then repeated, "What trip?"

Travis's gaze lingered on hers a moment longer before his concern faded. In its place, delight spread from his eyes like ripples in a pond. "You'll love this." He grinned. "We rent buses and take the entire Little League to a real major league baseball game. This year the visitors are the Norfolk Cannons, my old organization. I'll take the Sluggers down onto the field, introduce them to some of the players. It's a once-in-a-lifetime opportunity for the boys. An event like this doesn't happen at the snap of your fingers, though. We'll be working on it throughout the season."

Just in case there was a single chance in the world she hadn't heard him correctly, she asked again. "And this is to...?"

"Twister Stadium in Orlando. The Twisters are the newest team in the Eastern Division. Their stadium is beyond awesome. The kids will have a blast. You will, too."

No. I won't.

Travis was asking the impossible. "I can't make it," she managed, her voice tight.

Disappointment and determination battled in the dark eyes that met hers. "I know you don't like sports, but couldn't you pretend? For just one day? For the boys?"

If he'd chosen any other field in the nation, she might have risked it. She could have planned on getting lost in the crowd. But not there. Not where she'd been betrayed in the worst possible way. Travis might think he had everything figured out, but she absolutely was not going to Twister Stadium.

Defiant, she rose to face him. Her arms crossed, she tipped her face to tell him so.

Suddenly, squaring off with Travis didn't seem like her best move as a wave of longing shuddered from her throat straight down to her toes. She told herself she had to break the connection. Had to look away. Instead, she drank in Travis's clean, manly scent. She studied his smooth brow, the tiny lines at the corners of his eyes, the slope of his nose. It took every ounce of her willpower to wrench her gaze upward, but up was no good either. A smoldering interest filled the eyes that locked on to hers.

Courtney licked her lips.

She was so lost in Travis's gaze that she flinched when a serious wail rose from the baby monitor. The door at the top of the stairs popped open.

"Mom! Addie pooped her diapers," Josh shouted.

"Be right there." Courtney ducked away from the man who looked as dazed as she felt. Knowing she'd have to be the one to get them moving in the right direction, she cleared her throat.

"Looks like we're out of time. Unless you want to volunteer for diaper duty…"

"No—no, that's all right," he stammered.

She hid a grin when he bolted for the door. As he neared it, his feet slowed and, along with them, so did her heart. At the last possible second, he turned around.

"We aren't done here, you and I." He wagged his finger between them. "I'll be by in the morning. We'll pick this up again."

Before she had a chance to disagree, he was out the door. As she watched his tall frame disappear down the street, she shook her head. In a coffee shop that would, hopefully, be filled with customers, there wouldn't be time to chat with the hunky baseball coach. No matter how much she wanted to. Or how often she told herself it was a bad idea.

That night as she tucked him into bed, Josh reached up to give her a hug. "Mom, thanks," he whispered.

"You had a good day, huh?" Courtney teased. "Even though you had to do your homework?"

Josh scrunched his nose. "Not that part. For saying I could play Little League. I'm glad Coach Oak picked me for his team."

"You know," she said, smoothing the sheet under Josh's chin, "he talked Principal Morgan into letting you play so you could stay in school. Coach Oak didn't have to do that, but he thinks you can be a good player." She took a breath. "I think you can be good at a lot of things. You could be a doctor. Or a builder. Or even a cowboy. There's a world of possibilities open to you, as long as you do well in school." She kissed his nose. "So buckle down and study, okay?"

"Okay, Mom," he said through a yawn. He flopped onto his stomach. A muffled question rose from beneath the blankets. "Mom, why do cowboys have to study?"

Courtney thought fast. "They have to know what's wrong when their horses get sick. See you in the morning, honey."

At the door, she paused to take another look at the boy who'd recently shown glimpses of his happier former self. The talk she'd had with him on Thursday had helped effect the change, but she couldn't ignore another truth. So had Travis. He'd gone out of his way to help her son, and for that she was grateful. But no matter how much she appreciated the way he'd taken Josh under his wing, she wouldn't count on the coach any more than she had to.

Not even for the little things.

Chapter Five

At seven in the morning, birds chirped in the trees that lined the main streets of Cocoa Village. Security gates remained locked in place in front of closed shops. With few of the parking spaces occupied, Travis pulled to the curb in front of Coffee on Brevard.

From the sidewalk, he stopped to watch a boat head out from the city docks. Its prow cut through the fog-blanketed river. He inhaled deeply…and exhaled just as quickly. The salty air smelled fishier than it had the day before. He tucked the worn leather glove deeper under his arm and kept moving.

Inside he caught the glance Courtney aimed at him when the bell over the door jingled. She paused serving the next person in line only long enough for the briefest of smiles, but it was enough to give him a tiny jolt. He sputtered to a halt, his thoughts jumbled.

He knew he should go. He wasn't moving.

He thrust his hands into his pockets and faced the truth. He'd been drawn to Courtney from the moment he'd first seen her. The warnings he'd given himself to stay away from the "needy" widow and her troubled son hadn't worked. Besides, nothing about the single mom screamed for help. In fact, her fierce independence and determination were part of what he found so attractive.

That and a body that made him think about moving from first base to second to…

Not that he was going to slide into home, or even go to bat. He considered Addie's sweet smile, Josh's attitude. No doubt about it, they'd be better off with someone who was in it for the long haul…and that wasn't him.

"Busy place," he noted, stepping to the counter as the last person in line headed for the condiment stand. Determined not to fall under Courtney's spell, he avoided her eyes by pointing to nearby tables where people lingered over their coffee. "Is it usually like this?"

She swiped a sponge over the counter. "About normal for a Monday. People were waiting when I opened this morning."

Keeping his focus on the view beyond the window was tougher than he expected when she smiled so widely that dimples graced her cheeks. He gave it his best shot. "You'd think business would be down on the days when so many of the shops are closed, wouldn't you?"

She turned toward the mammoth brew station and began wiping down spigots. "The owners use Mondays to catch up on inventory and restock after the weekend." She turned, holding a pot aloft. "Can I treat you to a cup? House blend? Or Kona mocha?"

"Either's fine, thanks. How about adding a couple of pastries, too." He slipped a few dollars from his wallet and slid the money across. Aware that avoiding Courtney altogether offered the best solution, he drew in a breath. "I didn't stop to consider how much work it takes to run a business when I asked you to be the Sluggers' team mom," he began. "Maybe it's too much to ask."

A shadow flickered in her eyes.

"Backing out of our deal already?"

"I'm not saying that. I'm simply giving you a way out if you want it."

Her hand settled over the bills. "I called the parents last night. They've all signed up for their shifts in the concession stand and such. There are only one or two holes left in the schedule. I can fill in if no one volunteers."

"You spoke to everyone?" Travis shook his head. Not even Marty's mom had been that efficient.

Courtney slipped two glistening sweet rolls onto a stark white plate. "If we get pant and shirt sizes at practice on Tuesday, we'll have the uniforms in time for team pictures."

He blew a breath across his cup and took a sip. The hot coffee landed in his stomach, where it spread a satisfying warmth. "So, where are the kids?"

"Addie's taking a nap in the office." Courtney motioned toward a door at the back of the dining area. "Josh left for the bus stop just before you got here."

"That's early, isn't it?" Orange Blossom's first bell wouldn't ring for another hour.

"The bus route runs all along the river and back." Her expression turned pensive. "It's impossible to carpool. Not with the shop."

Normally, he wasn't much of a caffeine addict, but he suspected daily trips to Coffee on Brevard could easily become a part of his routine. Should he offer to give the boy a lift to school? Not if he intended to keep his distance.

To stop himself from saying words he had no business speaking, Travis bit into one of the cinnamon buns.

Sugar exploded on his tongue while Courtney eyed him as if she wasn't sure why he was standing there. He swallowed hastily and held out the glove.

"I brought this." He'd hoped to give it to Josh himself so the boy would know someone was there for him, the same way his high school baseball coach had taken a life-altering interest in him after his folks' divorce. A former professional athlete himself, Coach Marsden had inspired Travis to follow in his footsteps.

She eyed the battered leather as if it had strings attached. "Are you sure? What if something happens to it?"

As he met her troubled gaze, Travis felt off balance. He hurried to reassure them both that the earth hadn't shifted beneath their feet.

"Hey, it's just an old glove. It's been sitting in my closet for years. Might as well let the boy put it to good use."

At last Courtney sighed and reached for the scuffed and stained leather. Their fingers brushed as she took it. The touch sent a pleasant shudder through him, and her soft inhale told him she felt the same thing. Smiling, he watched her spin away and tuck the glove beneath the counter.

"I'll make sure you get it back," she said, turning to face him again. "When the business is a little more stable, I'll buy Josh one of his own. In the meantime, he'll be thrilled. And you—" she paused "—your coffee is on the house for as long as you want."

A glance at the clock on the back wall reminded him that Josh wasn't the only one who had to be at school on time.

"I'd hoped we could start laying the groundwork for

the trip to Twister Stadium this morning, but I have a staff meeting. Catch you tomorrow?"

The same dismay he'd read in her eyes before reappeared.

"About that..." she began.

"Whatever it is," he said, cautiously placing his hand atop hers, "we'll work it out, okay?"

Her eyes widened, though this time neither of them flinched. Certain they'd made progress but uncertain where they were headed or if he even wanted to go there, Travis reluctantly retrieved his hand.

"I'll see you at practice tomorrow night?" she asked.

"Oh, I'll be back for coffee before then," he countered. The trip to Twister Stadium really did involve a lot of planning. Besides, he suspected a certain pretty widow might be even more addictive than the caffeine she served.

TUESDAY, COURTNEY POURED a handful of Cheerios onto Addie's stroller tray. Immediately entranced, the little girl began scooting the round circles from one end to the other. Occasionally she stopped to fist one into her mouth.

While her daughter played with her snack, Courtney set up a folding chair and spread a blanket on the grass beyond the dugout. She eyed the other parents. For the most part, mothers with older children chose seats in the metal bleachers while the fathers leaned against the low chain-link fence that ran from behind first base to the edge of the outfield. A brisk breeze brought snippets of their conversation.

"We hit the batting cages every night...."

"Andy's control is much better this year...."

"Have you seen the new kids?"

At this last, she stopped pulling Addie's toys from the diaper bag and listened more closely. Would the other parents accept Josh as one of the team? Or would they complain that Travis had drafted a kid who'd never played baseball before? As much as she'd fought against letting her son play for the Sluggers, she wouldn't stand quietly on the sidelines and see him ostracized. Not by anyone.

"Sluggers rule!"

The voices of a dozen ten- to twelve-year-olds rose in a communal shout from the parking lot. She lifted Addie as the noise caught the attention of every parent on the field. They stood, applauding as a thundering herd of boys and their coaches raced down the small hill. Tension bled from Courtney's shoulders when she spotted Josh, dressed in baseball pants and wearing his new cleats.

In the middle of the group, her son looked as though he fit right in.

Focused on Josh, she didn't notice that Travis had stopped beside her. By the time she did, he stood so close she could pick out individual hairs in the faint stubble that graced his cheeks. He tickled Addie under the chin until the baby chortled.

"Walk over to the stands with me," he said. "I want to introduce you as the new team mom."

All too aware of his masculine presence, she fell in step beside Travis as he led them to the bleachers.

"I see some new faces and a lot of familiar ones," he said while behind them one of the assistant coaches took the team through a few warm-up exercises. "I'm confident that the Sluggers will have a great season."

A father she hadn't met gave a rousing cheer. Travis held up one hand, a signal for silence.

"The same rules apply this year as last but, for our new folks, I'll repeat them. Practices are here at Orange Blossom. Make sure the boys arrive on time. On game days, they'll need to be at McLarty Park an hour early. Parents, you're welcome to attend all activities and cheer for the team. In fact, I encourage it as long as you keep your comments positive and supportive."

Courtney wasn't sure, but she thought Travis let his gaze linger on specific individuals when he said, "Remember to exercise the same sportsmanship we're trying to teach your children. No razzing the other teams, their players or their coaches. Absolutely no arguing with the umpires."

The warm weight of Travis's hand landed on her shoulder. He shot her a wicked grin.

"This here is Courtney Smith and sweet little Addie." With his free hand, Travis gave the baby a playful poke. "Courtney has volunteered to act as team mom this season. I'm going to turn things over to her now since—" he threw a look behind him "—it seems there's a practice I need to lead."

He gave her arm a squeeze that sent ripples of awareness through her. Stunned by the reaction and knowing there was only so much a woman could take and still maintain her composure, Courtney turned to the parents. They waited attentively for her to say…something.

"Hi." She shifted Addie on her hip. "You'll have to forgive me if I can't match names with faces just yet. You've all been great about signing up to work the concession stand. If anyone wants to take an extra shift, we have a couple of openings left to fill. I've printed up schedules, but they're—" she patted Addie's rounded bottom "—still in this little one's diaper bag. If you could all stop by, I'll be sitting over there."

She gestured toward the trees but swore no one noticed. Oh, one or two of the parents gave vacant nods. Melinda, the woman she'd met at tryouts, sent her a cheery look. Courtney returned her half wave and turned to see what had captured everyone's attention.

As she suspected, Travis was the culprit.

On the field, he moved with a lithe grace from player to player, positioning them for infield practice. When he squatted down to speak face-to-face with the catcher, Courtney swore she heard one of the mothers swoon. The fathers— Well, if the starry-eyed hero worship in their eyes was any indication, they'd all become members of the Travis Oak Fan Club.

A club she was just as determined not to join.

The coach might be the adored answer to the other parents' prayers, but she was not going to fall under his spell. First and foremost, he was a baseball player, and she was done with those.

On her way back to her chair, Courtney inhaled her baby's sweet scent and let the memories of the past year wash over her. Betrayal and devastating loss battled any attraction to another athlete. The circumstances surrounding Ryan's death alone had almost driven her insane. Would have if she hadn't been so caught up in tending to a distraught son and a newborn. She couldn't risk going down that road again.

"Mama!" Addie squirmed in an embrace that was admittedly tighter than usual. "Plu-ay!"

"Oh, you want to play, do you?" Blinking away her tears, Courtney leaned in to steal a kiss. She summoned up a smile. "All right. Let's bounce." She jostled the baby on one knee and chanted, "Pat-a-cake, pat-a-cake, baker's man."

Addie's little face scrunched into a delighted wreath. "Pa-cake." She clapped her tiny hands.

The activities on the field faded into the background while she played with the baby. By the time Addie had tired of the games and was snuggled into her stroller with a bottle, Travis stood at home plate. His back to her, he hit grounders to the boys he'd positioned around the bases while the assistant coaches worked with another set of players in the field beyond.

Perplexed when she didn't see Josh in the outfield, Courtney spotted her son smack-dab between second and third base at shortstop. Though starting an inexperienced player at a demanding infield position wasn't what she'd expected, she shrugged her concerns aside. Decisions like that were up to the coach. She'd have to trust that he knew what he was doing.

The thought stopped her.

Did she really trust Travis? On any level?

Part of her said she should. After all, he'd shown Josh nothing but kindness from the moment he'd intervened in the school principal's office. The way he'd dealt with her son at tryouts had renewed her hope that her angry preteen would conquer his demons. Then there was the glove Travis had lent the boy. She'd thought it was a discard, something left behind by another player. Finding the coach's name in the worn cotton lining had shocked her so badly her mouth had gaped open.

What kind of man lent souvenirs of his own childhood to a kid he barely knew?

She tugged on the end of her ponytail as she tried to

figure out what motivated Travis. Was he simply reaching out, feeling sorry for a child who'd lost his dad? Or was it something more? Did he see her son as the next baseball phenom?

Relief washed through her when Josh let a slow grounder get past him like no prodigy she'd ever seen. He chased after the ball.

"Sorry, Coach," he called as he scooped the bouncing ball into his glove and hustled to make the throw to Travis.

"It's okay. Just stay with it, man," Travis called.

Courtney shaded her eyes and stared. She'd been around far too many baseball coaches. Every single one had harped on the mistakes their players made. The tall man standing at this plate praised the kids for making good moves. As for their errors, she watched as Travis walked the third baseman through a muffed routine play. The way the young coach handled it, she thought the kid stood a good chance of learning from the experience.

"Okay, let's take a ten-minute break." Travis called all the players in from the field. "Grab some water. Then we'll scrimmage for a while before we call it quits for the day."

Boys streamed off the field and into the dugout, the plastic cleats on the bottoms of their shoes echoing against the hard cement floor. For the next few minutes, Courtney was inundated by parents who took advantage of the interruption to pick up schedules and drop off information about uniforms. When she looked up again, Tommy Markham stood on the pitcher's mound and his mother was on approach.

"You don't mind if I sit with you, do you?" Melinda unfolded a chair without waiting for an answer. "I don't like to sit with the *other* parents when Tommy pitches. I'm too nervous. Don't know why. He always does great. Just *great*." Plastic webbing groaned as she collapsed into her seat.

"I'm glad to have the company." Courtney checked on Addie. The baby had finished her bottle but seemed content in the stroller.

"You probably don't realize it, but Tommy is going to play pro ball one day."

"It's a bit early to start making career plans, isn't it?" Courtney stole a look at the thin shoulders of youngsters who hadn't yet reached puberty. The boys had years of growing to do before they became draft eligible upon graduation from high school.

"My husband says you can't start soon enough. We're already looking at colleges with the best baseball programs. But that's only an option. Tommy will probably go from high school straight into the pros."

"You must be doing something better than I am." Courtney gave her head a rueful shake. "I can't imagine Josh handling that kind of pressure at eighteen or nineteen. And all that time on the road? It's terribly hard on both players and their families."

If she heeded the warning, Melinda gave no sign of it. She leaned forward, concentrating on her son as Tommy went into his windup.

Courtney watched the twelve-year-old lob several pitches toward home plate. Other than carrot-colored hair and a toothy grin, the boy looked completely average. Average height. Average weight. Worse, he was right-handed, a trait that wouldn't earn him a second look in a sport that valued lefties.

Sensing disappointment in her friend's future, Courtney leaned back in her chair and steered the conversation away from the field.

"What have you been up to since the tryouts?"

"Shopping for the perfect dress." Melinda winced when Tommy's last practice pitch sailed in too high for a strike. "Haven't found it yet, but I won't give up till I do."

"Oh? A special occasion?" The first batter stepped to the plate, where he took a few practice swings. Courtney spotted Josh riding the pine in the visitors' dugout.

Melinda pivoted from the waist. "For the Little League fund-raiser. You *are* coming, aren't you?"

Courtney brushed a hand over her hair. "I doubt I'll make it." Given the current state of her bank account, the idea of spending extra money had *dumb move* written all over it. "I'm not sure I can afford to hire someone to watch the kids. Between the registration fees and equipment Josh needed, I'm pretty much tapped out."

"Oh, that's easy enough to fix." Melinda dismissed the problem with a wave of one hand. "We'll share a babysitter. I've already lined one up. I'm sure she'll just love Addie."

For half a second, Courtney indulged in a trip down memory lane. Back when she'd been the wife of a somebody, an evening event meant a touch-up at the hair salon, maybe a half day at the spa and her choice of designer dresses. Today only the simplest of those gowns hung in her closet, and she hadn't seen a stylist in months. But a night that didn't involve coffeepots or children did sound like something just this side of heaven. Besides, the event might bring more attention to Coffee on Brevard.

"Think anyone would mind if I handed out a few business cards?"

"Not at all," Melinda answered. Her attention shifted

to the field, where another pitcher had replaced Tommy on the mound. "Oh, Josh is up to bat." She reached out. "Now, don't worry if he struggles at the plate. He has to start somewhere."

Courtney eyed the hand that had given hers a consoling pat. She tucked her own fingers into her lap. Unless she'd totally missed the mark, Josh had inherited his father's raw talent. With a little bit of coaching and some practice, he'd soon be playing as well as any member of his team. Maybe better.

As if to prove her point, Josh batted the first pitch over the third baseman's head.

"Would you look at that!" Melinda exclaimed. "The pro scouts will have two Sluggers to watch this year." She peered at Courtney. "What does Josh want to be when he gets older?"

Anything but a baseball player.

Courtney hedged. "At this age his plans change almost daily. He's never played before. I doubt he'll stick with it."

And he wouldn't if she had anything to say about it.

"Looks like practice is about over," Melinda said after each squad had three chances at bat. She folded her chair and stood. "I'll see you Thursday?"

"Sounds good." Courtney nodded. For the next month, the team would practice every other day. She bent to store Addie's toys while she waited for Josh.

"He did better than I thought he would today."

At Travis's voice, Courtney straightened from the stroller. "Thanks." She paused, then added a nearly silent "I think."

A sweat-damped jersey pulled tight across Travis's chest when his weight shifted. He tugged his hat from his head and ran a hand through his hair. "He seems to like it. Are you okay with that?"

"I have to be, don't I?" She drew in a deep breath. She'd struck a deal and intended to keep her side of the bargain. She waited, wishing the coach would move along before she did or said something that would let him know how much she was attracted to him. To her dismay, he lingered at her side.

"Hey, Josh," he said, not missing a beat when her son neared. "How'd you like the glove?"

"It catches real good, Coach." The boy pantomimed the ball landing in the pocket and slapped one hand over it as if to keep it in place.

"From the way you hit today, I'd say you're improving there already." He gave Josh's hat brim a tug, then turned to the stroller. "And how's Miss Addie tonight?" He tickled the baby's chin.

The move elicited a laugh but, suddenly shy, Addie buried her head against the cushion.

"Well, I better let you guys get on home." He dusted his hands on his shorts. "I'm going to hit some before I call it a night." Travis pointed toward the field, where a bucket of baseballs stood at home plate. "Besides—" he aimed a thumb toward Josh "—I imagine this one's hungry."

Josh rubbed his stomach. "Mighty hungry, Mom."

The comment put Courtney's feet in motion. Herding her brood up the hill to the car, she called a quick "See you at the next practice" over her shoulder.

By the time she strapped Addie into her car seat and loaded the stroller into the trunk, Travis had stepped up to the plate. He grabbed one of the balls from the bucket, tossed it into the air and smacked it into center field. Courtney wrenched her eyes away from the strain of powerful muscles. She absolutely refused to stare at slim hips that twisted as Travis sent another ball flying. She wouldn't.

Well, just one more.

A metallic *crack* sounded through the night air.

"Mom, can we stop to eat on the way home?"

Courtney licked her lips and mumbled, "No. We're having fish sticks for supper."

Tearing her eyes from the field, she spotted her son making the kind of face mothers all over the world had learned to ignore. She thrust the key into the ignition. She turned it and was rewarded with...nothing but a click.

The engine, unlike her heart, didn't even try to turn over.

TRAVIS REACHED INTO the bucket and grabbed another ball. A short upward thrust sent it straight over his head. He timed the downward arc, swinging the bat in a dance he'd long since perfected.

Toss. Snap. Contact.

The ball sailed well beyond the reach of the tallest infielder. It bounced, then rolled across the grass behind first base. *Damn.* He'd wanted to put that one in center field. He rolled his shoulders and began again.

Why he felt the need to take his frustrations out on a bat and a ball, he wasn't quite sure. The team, his usual concern at this point in the season, didn't merit a second thought. His returning players had retained most of their knowledge over the nine months since they'd last run out onto the field together. Some of the boys had even attended midwinter camps in nearby Viera.

He tossed another ball and smacked it into left field.

Had he encouraged his team to invest too much in baseball? While he was glad they'd shown an interest beyond
Little League, he wouldn't want to raise false hopes.
None of the boys would ever make it to the pros. In
fact, only one of them even had a whisper of a chance.
He suspected Josh possessed that rare combination of
natural talent and physical strength that put him heads
above the average player. Yet he'd never stepped onto a
field before tryouts.

What kind of father didn't teach his child to swing a
bat, field a ball?

Travis shook his head in disbelief. Josh was outgo-
ing, eager to learn, passionate about baseball. Any man
would be proud to call him son. Any man worth his salt,
that was. But according to Courtney, Josh's dad hadn't
shown much interest in the boy.

As the curvy little blonde invaded his thoughts, Travis's bat sliced cleanly through the chill evening air. The
ball thudded onto the red clay at his feet.

Women! He tapped the bat against his cleats.

He whiffed the next ball and groaned. He harped on
the boys, telling them to concentrate on the plays, on hitting, on the game. Yet here he was, unable to focus long
enough for batting practice.

The bat he dropped landed in the dirt beside his glove.
Jogging out to the field, he retrieved the balls he'd managed to hit. One by one, he dropped them into the five-
gallon bucket. When it was full, he grabbed his gear and
headed for the parking lot.

Forcing himself to dwell on nothing more than a
shower and a good meal, Travis made it to the top of the
hill before he spotted the raised hood of a car in the lot.
He squinted at the compact figure leaning over the en-

gine. His gut twisted at the plaintive wail that rose from the backseat. He covered the ground quickly, unable to stop his legs from taking longer strides than necessary.

"Need some help?" he asked the moment he came within speaking distance.

Courtney straightened. One hand perched on a slim hip, she let out an audible sigh. "Know anything about cars?"

"A bit. Let me put this away." He hefted the bucket and watched as her eyes tracked the movement.

From the Jeep's storage compartment, he grabbed a wrench, a rag and a flashlight. His hand hesitated over the cooler he kept stocked with Gatorade and water.

"The kids want something to drink?" he called over one shoulder.

"Yes!" came Josh's immediate reply.

"That'd be great," Courtney added.

Carrying a couple of bottles, he loped back the way he'd come.

While Courtney made quick work of dispensing the drinks to her children—Addie's in a sippy cup—he studied the open engine compartment. "Here, hold this," he said when she stood beside him again. Torn between awareness of her and the youngsters in the car, he made sure to avoid contact as he handed her the flashlight.

"Shine that over here." He ran his fingers along the belts, searching for tears. "They're a little worn, but they aren't broken," he said a minute later. He checked the fluid levels and cable connections. "So far, so good. Why don't you give her a try and see what happens."

The car sank the tiniest bit when Courtney slid behind the wheel. Moments later he heard a click and then silence.

Travis wiped his hands on the towel he'd tucked into his waistband. "Sounds like the battery. Could be the alternator or something else, but that's where I'd bet my money."

Courtney rounded the car to stand beside him. "Okay," she said tentatively. "Does that mean I need a tow truck?"

He noted her troubled frown. "Not necessarily. I'll jump you."

Her head canted. Wisps of hair fell forward, and Travis curled his fingers, fighting the urge to brush the tendrils from her face. He had no doubt that Courtney's whispered "I bet you say that to all the girls" was meant for his ears alone.

"Not as many as you might think," he answered. With the raised hood shielding them, he met and held her gaze. "And none for quite some time," he added, his voice low.

An urge he fought to deny swept him when her tongue darted out to moisten her lips. One gesture, the slightest shift toward her, and he knew she'd step into his embrace. His grip on the wrench tightened. He took a step back.

Standing in the middle of a parking lot in front of a broken-down car and with her two kids fussing in the backseat, yeah. Talk about bad timing.

"Hold on. I have a pair of cables in the Jeep." Turning, he used the reprieve to get his libido under control.

At her side once more, he glanced her way. Gone was the starry-eyed gaze that had transformed her expression only seconds earlier. He bent to the job at hand. A couple of swipes of his rag cleaned the battery connections. He attached the cables, red first, then black. Sliding behind the wheel of the Jeep, he cranked it up and let the engine run.

"Okay, now, when I say 'Go,' start your engine," he

called to Courtney. He watched while she got into position. "Go."

The aging sedan roared to life.

He crossed to her door. Leaning down, he braced his arms on her window frame. "Leave it in Park. You'll need to let it run for a few minutes."

From behind the wheel, where she was safely out of reach, Courtney peered up at him. "For a baseball player, you know your way around cars."

"Self-preservation." Travis raised one shoulder and let it drop. "Everybody thinks you make it to the pros, you're in the money. But players in the minor leagues don't earn much. To get by, I learned which diners served the biggest helpings at the cheapest price and taught myself how to handle routine car maintenance. All that would have changed if I'd made it to the Show, but…" He shrugged again. "Never did."

"Well, thanks for this. Who knows how long we'd have been stuck here."

Courtney's hand brushed his. The jolt of electricity that shot through him had nothing to do with jumper cables or batteries. It was all Courtney.

From the backseat, Addie raised another squall that turned his insides to mush. Pulling away from the car, he straightened.

"Sounds like she could use some dinner." He squelched an offer to take them out for burgers. Getting even more tied up with Courtney and her family was exactly what he did not need to do.

"The car's okay to drive now?"

Was that longing in her blue eyes? In the gloom of the darkened sky, it was hard to tell.

"I'll follow you," he said before he could stop himself.

He swallowed and argued that he was only making sure her vehicle didn't die and leave her stranded on a busy street. His gut told him it was more than that.

Even when he was back in his own driver's seat and safely out of touching distance, Courtney still exerted a pull on him. He followed her car's taillights and knew he was doomed. No matter how much he told himself it was a bad idea, he couldn't deny the part of him that wanted to give a relationship with the perky blonde a chance.

Careful, now.

He didn't want to be *that guy,* the one who hurt Josh and Addie, when he left for Norfolk or wherever the Cannons sent him. Especially not after what the children had already been through. His mom had had a boyfriend or two. Eventually, they'd disappeared, which had been as difficult for him and his brother as it had been for her.

When Courtney pulled to a stop in front of Coffee on Brevard, he was no closer to deciding how to proceed than he'd been at the field. But helping out was in his nature, so he reached into the glove box and pulled out a business card from a man whose son used to play for the Sluggers.

"Here," he said, handing it to her moments later. "Bill runs an auto repair shop up on U.S. 1. He'll give you the team price on a new battery."

And with that, Travis walked away knowing he should leave the rest up to Courtney but equally certain he wouldn't.

Chapter Six

"Mom, Coach Oak is here."

Courtney looked up from the fresh diaper she was sliding beneath her daughter's bare bottom.

Travis?

Hurriedly, she tugged Addie's little legs into a clean pair of overalls and gave the baby a quick hug. She set Addie in her walker and watched the little girl scoot down the hall.

Courtney glanced down. She looked a fright in an old pair of jeans and a T-shirt. A mix of curiosity and indignation swirled through her. Whatever had brought Travis to her door on a school night, she hoped it was important.

Fingers crossed, she followed in Addie's wake. Her pace slowed to a halt at the end of the hall, where she took in the scene before her. Her lips parted.

In the small but tidy living room, Travis sat on the couch talking baseball with Josh while Addie gazed adoringly up at them. The scene was the one Courtney had always envisioned for her children, but being married to a superstar had meant sacrifices, compromises. Family life had been one of them. Watching Travis with her children, she fought a wave of nostalgia for the good old days that had never been.

Seconds later the coach glanced up from his conversation with Josh, met her gaze and winked. The move broke the spell and propelled her into the room. The minute her heels sounded on the hardwood floor, her daughter swung toward her.

"Co-Oak." Addie beamed a toothless grin.

"Coach Oak," Courtney repeated to her clearly besotted little girl.

Travis rose, his impressive size taking up too much space and absorbing far too much of the oxygen in the tiny room.

"I ran into Bill Jessup after school. He said you didn't bring your car into his shop. Thought I'd see if you needed another jump start."

She eyed the man who had to bend slightly to avoid knocking his head on the slanted ceiling. He could fool the kids, even lie to himself, but he wasn't fooling her. More than the sad state of car repairs had driven him to climb the stairs to her apartment over the store. And while she appreciated the handsome man's interest— what girl wouldn't?—she was pretty sure encouraging him belonged on the Top-Ten List of Bad Ideas.

She forced a little coolness into her voice. "I wasn't quite ready to do that."

"Oh?" The question came without a challenge. "Bill's running a sale right now. You'll never get a lower price. Or better service."

Absently, she smoothed her T-shirt. Taking care of the car seemed like the smart thing to do…unless your checkbook was running on fumes.

As if he sensed her hesitation, Travis gestured toward Josh and Addie. "If you get stranded, next time I might not be around to help out." He offered her a sheepish grin.

It was hard to find fault with his logic. She needed reliable transportation. Small towns like Cocoa Village didn't offer bus service, and taxis were too expensive for routine errands like the ones she made to the big-box store for supplies. She let her hands drop to her sides.

"You're right about the car. It wouldn't turn over this afternoon. Let me pull some things together, and if you're sure you don't mind…"

"Not at all."

Courtney turned to her son. "Josh, bring the book you're reading for your book report." To her self-appointed white knight, she said, "Let me grab Addie's diaper bag and my purse, and we'll be all set."

Following Travis through the streets of Cocoa Village and across the causeway to Merritt Island a few minutes later, she tried telling herself it made sense to accept the man's help. He obviously wanted Josh to play for the Sluggers as much as she wanted her boy to stay in school.

But was she making a huge mistake by letting Travis get close to her? Courtney tightened her grip on the steering wheel. To her children? Their emotional well-being was every bit as important as their physical safety. So why was she even thinking of Travis? The man lived and breathed baseball. And that was a deal breaker, wasn't it?

She was still trying to figure out the answers when Travis pulled into the parking lot beneath a gigantic sign advertising Bill's Discount Auto Repair. By the time she unbuckled her seat belt, he held her door open for her. At her side, he guided her little family into a store where the smell of new rubber competed with oil and grease.

"Welcome to Bill's Dis—"

The man behind the counter stopped talking as he looked up and spotted the new arrivals. "Travis! Glad to see you could make it! What can I do for my favorite baseball player?" Dressed in stained overalls, the burly figure stepped toward them offering his hand.

Expecting him to spend the next few minutes reminiscing with Travis about his days in the minor leagues, Courtney moved aside. The touch of Travis's hand at the small of her back halted her flight and nudged her forward.

"Bill, this is Courtney Smith. Her son, Josh, is one of our new Sluggers this year."

"Ms. Smith. Josh. And this little one?" Bill grinned at the baby.

"Addie," Courtney offered as her daughter buried her face.

"Addie," repeated Bill. "Welcome to Bill's Discount, where prices are low and quality is high. What can I do for you today?"

She tilted her head, pleased when Travis stepped back and let her take the lead. She explained the problem, then asked, "Do you have time to take a look at it?"

Bill's voice boomed. "I'd be happy to. If I could have your keys?"

She placed them in his calloused palm.

"Back in a jiff," he said before disappearing through a door behind the counter.

In a matter of minutes, he returned with news.

"One of the cells in your battery is dry. You aren't pulling enough current to start the car. Let me show you what we have to choose from. Our top-of-the-line model comes with a sixty-month guarantee…."

The little she understood about the inner workings of a car could be crammed into a coffee cup with plenty of room for cream and sugar. To make things worse, Addie demanded attention, insisting she play peekaboo while Bill talked. Before he'd moved on to his second choice, Courtney bobbed her head without following a word the mechanic said.

"Here." Travis held out his hands. "Why don't I take Addie and Josh next door to McDonald's while you two sort things out."

"If she'll go with you. She can be a bit stubborn." Hesitantly, Courtney handed the baby off, then waited, fully expecting her daughter to scream bloody murder.

From her new perch in Travis's arms, Addie gave a wide-eyed look that all but demanded to know why she hadn't been there before.

Travis laughed. "Well, I guess we're all right, then." He clapped a hand on Josh's shoulder. "How 'bout it? Shall we go grab a booth while your mom handles things?"

"Sure, Coach." Her son peered up at her through soulful eyes. "Mom, can I have a hamburger? I'm *starving*." As if on cue, his stomach rumbled.

Courtney shook her head. The new battery was going to put another dent in a balance that needed a rapid infusion of cash. She opened her mouth, intending to tell her son they couldn't afford to eat at a restaurant, even if it was only fast food.

"Um, I—"

"I'm a mite peckish, too," Travis interrupted. "How 'bout we make this my treat—paybacks for all those free cups of coffee you've served me in the mornings."

He'd made fewer than a half dozen stops by Coffee on Brevard. Each time, he'd nursed a single cup. Not that she'd argue with the man. Not in front of her children. And especially not after he'd gone out of his way to help her.

"Okay," she said, though she sent Josh a meaningful glance. "But don't overdo it."

"Can Addie have French fries?" Travis wanted to know.

Courtney sighed. Having given in this far, she figured she might as well surrender completely. "She eats more ketchup than fries, but yes."

Watching Travis herd her children through the door, she felt a pang of remorse so deep it took her breath away. What if she'd married someone who honestly liked children, chose to spend his days around them, set himself up as a role model for them? Though she knew it was a waste of time, she had to ask if things would have turned out differently. Would she still lie awake nights worrying what kind of man her son would become? If he'd battle the same demons his father had fought? And what about Addie? She'd never even known Ryan. How would not knowing her father affect her?

She shook the troubling thoughts from her head and turned to Bill. "Now, about my car. You were saying…"

In the end, she grudgingly pulled out the credit card she kept for absolute emergencies. Walking into McDonald's a short time later, she steeled herself against a mouth-watering aroma. Instead, she stopped at the counter long enough to buy a Diet Coke with the loose change from the bottom of her purse. She took a sip. At a booth near the back, she spotted Josh, the remains of a Happy Meal spread out on the table before him. Oddly enough, he'd devoured the apple slices first and now munched on a hamburger. Across from him Travis fed bite-size pieces of apple to Addie from her own colorful kid-sized box while his food sat untouched on the table.

Something twisted deep in her stomach.

She couldn't deny how much her kids needed a male influence in their lives. And there sat Travis, doing all the things she'd learned to never expect from a man who lived his life on a diamond. She squared her shoulders, slid onto the seat beside Josh and snagged one of his fries.

"Hey."

Dipping the purloined potato in ketchup, she ignored her son's good-natured protest and took a steadying breath.

"Travis, thanks for everything."

One solid shoulder rose and fell in a careless shrug. Courtney let her eyes drink her fill of the man on the opposite side of the table. Did he have any idea how endearing he looked sitting there feeding sliced fruit to her daughter?

Travis slid a colorful box her way. "This was Addie's. I wasn't sure if she liked burgers or not. My nieces didn't start eating them till they were a bit older."

"Oh?" Courtney tipped the open box. Inside lay an unwrapped hamburger and a packet of fries. She claimed the latter to share with her daughter and pushed the rest aside while she dealt out questions. "How many do you have? Do they live nearby?"

The paper Travis unfolded around a Quarter Pounder crinkled. "My brother and his wife live in Tampa. They have two girls, seven and nine, and a boy who just turned three. Mom lives nearby and dotes on all of them." He aimed his chin toward her unwrapped sandwich. "If you're not going to eat that, Josh probably will."

"That leg of yours still hollow?" she asked her son.

The extra food disappeared from her hand almost before she had a chance to blink. "What do you say?"

"Thanks, Mom. Thanks, Coach." Josh tore into the burger as if he hadn't eaten in days instead of minutes.

Courtney chose a French fry. "That must be nice. Having family so close by."

"You don't?"

"No, it's just me and the kids. My folks separated while I was in college. Now they live on opposite sides of the country. Dad remarried a couple of years ago. His new family keeps him busy." Too busy to do more than fly out for Ryan's funeral.

The muscles in Travis's jaw worked briefly. "And your mother?"

"I guess you'd say she's not the type to bake cookies and knit sweaters." Courtney forced a laugh. "She moved to New York after the breakup. She spends her days shopping and her nights…" With an eye on the kids, she finished, "Let's just say she's still looking for the Fountain of Youth."

"Got it." Something that looked an awful lot like sympathy sparkled in Travis's eyes.

Courtney wanted to tell him there was nothing to feel sorry about. She couldn't blame her parents for living out their dreams any more than she'd accept criticism for the steps she'd taken to protect her family after Ryan died.

"Mom, can I go play now?"

Courtney glanced at her watch. In five minutes Josh had scarfed down his dinner and was ready for the next thing. "Where's the book you're supposed to be reading?"

A lopsided grin spread across the boy's face. "I think I might have left it in the car."

Courtney swallowed a sigh. Carefully, she scoured

the play area that jutted out from the restaurant. Behind clear glass walls, children dashed between painted tubes that were far too small to hide an adult. Satisfied that the area was safe, she nodded. "Okay, but just until the car is ready. The minute we get home, you get back to work."

Once Josh slid past her, she handed Addie a lone French fry.

"K-shup," the little one chirped.

"Want some ketchup?" she asked, dumping enough onto a folded wrapper to keep the child busy for some time. While Addie made every effort to gum the potato to death by repeatedly dunking it in the red goo, Courtney let her attention drift back to Travis.

Time to get to know more about the man who'd invaded their lives.

"Your brother, the one in Tampa, does he play baseball, too?"

"Not anymore. He was a catcher. Signed with UF but injured his back." Travis shrugged. "Later, he went into medicine. He and his wife are nurses at Tampa General."

Courtney brushed at a loose strand of hair. In the play area, Josh and another boy clung to climbing ropes, each doing his best to reach the top. She handed Addie another fry. "And you? What led you to Orange Blossom?"

"After I gave up the dream, I needed a job. Lucky for me, my degree in sports sciences included a teaching certificate. Bob, Principal Morgan, had an opening for a P.E. teacher." Travis took another bite and chewed thoughtfully before adding, "I have to admit, I like working with kids a lot more than I thought I would."

She studied the man who'd shown her son more kindness than she'd expected. "I sense a *but* in there somewhere."

Travis leaned back, his long legs stretched out beneath the seat beside her. His dark eyes bore into hers. "I've been talking to the Cannons about a coaching job."

Courtney caught her bottom lip between her teeth, but that didn't prevent sharp disappointment from knifing through her chest. "So," she breathed. "You're leaving."

"Not yet. Later this summer. Maybe."

"Soon enough."

The news was a game changer. She dredged another fry through the ketchup, concentrating on anything but Travis's broad features while she marshaled her own thoughts.

"I'm sure the town will miss you," she said once she was certain she'd stuffed the last of her feelings for the coach into a box and nailed the lid closed. "People here look up to you. Principal Morgan. The other parents. Even Bill." She aimed a glance toward the repair shop.

"Oh, that," he said as if playing the hero was old hat. "Lot of these dads, they have big dreams for their sons. I came closer to living out that fantasy than most anyone around here. That's what they're reacting to, not me." He aimed a thumb toward his chest. "Inside I'm not any better than the guy who fixes cars for a living."

She searched his eyes for any telltale smugness that would expose his false modesty. No matter how hard she looked, not a hint of conceit marred the brown depths. Intrigued, she held his gaze until her awareness of the room around them faded and there was nothing but Travis and his penetrating presence. A sudden wish to reach out to him stirred within her.

It took every ounce of her willpower, but she retreated. She couldn't risk getting closer to Travis than absolutely necessary. Especially now that she knew he wasn't going to stick around. When he grabbed a napkin to blot ketchup from Addie's lips, her decision wavered ever so slightly. But by the time her phone pinged with a text saying the car was done, she knew what she had to do.

"Thanks for seeing us out here. And for dinner." She stood, palming her cell phone so he could see the text from Bill. "The car's ready. Time to get these kids home. We have another big day tomorrow."

It was now or never. She had to put some space between her and a certain tall, dark and attractive baseball player. No matter how little she wanted to do it.

"ADDIE," COURTNEY CALLED. "You have to hold my hand whenever we're outside." Now that she'd taken her first steps, her daughter insisted on walking wherever they went. Her vocabulary expanded daily. She'd even started stringing words into simple sentences.

"Walk." Addie grinned and darted away, the rubber soles of her brother's hand-me-downs scuffing through the grass.

Startled, a bug sprang into the air.

"Mama." Clearly awed, the baby pointed. "Ye-ump!"

"Grasshopper. Now, hold my hand." Uncertain whether she was ready to face more challenges in a year that had held too many of them, Courtney wiggled her fingers. "We have to talk to Josh."

"Chosh." Addie toddled closer.

Slowly, they made their way across the open grassy area toward the bleachers where the Sluggers had gathered to wait for practice. Courtney beckoned her son away from the group.

"Let me see it," she said when he was close enough that she didn't have to shout.

"See what?" Josh asked with a nearly believable look of innocence.

"Don't play dumb. I want to see your spelling and the note from Ms. Culpepper." In the month since the draft, Josh had breathed, eaten and slept nothing but baseball. She'd worried that his grades might slip as a result, and at lunchtime his teacher had called to confirm her concerns.

Shoulders slumped, Josh slung his backpack onto the ground at Addie's feet.

"I can't now, Mom. I hafta put on my cleats and get on the field."

Courtney held up one hand. "Not so fast, mister. Papers first."

Showing a decided return of the attitude she'd hoped they'd banished, Josh mumbled under his breath. His posture stiff and unyielding, he unzipped his bag. He riffled through the contents, at last handing her several wrinkled pages.

Courtney sucked in a fortifying breath at the line of red Xs along one edge of the review sheet. "Oh, Josh," she whispered. His once average grades had taken a definite nosedive. She fought for control. "You told me you studied this morning. How'd you do that and still get so many wrong answers?"

"I didn't have time." The shrug her son gave barely shifted his thin shoulders. "Coach Oak gave us some exercises he said we had to do before school every day."

She rubbed her brow, where a headache threatened. She shouldn't be surprised. Josh had grown up watching his father's single-mindedness toward baseball. The boy had to have absorbed some of it. But the attitude that had once made Ryan a superstar had also spelled disaster for his home life. A fact she'd done her best to shield her children from.

Apparently, she'd done too good a job.

She scoured clear blue skies and puffy white clouds, hoping for the right words to help her son find the balance his father's life had been missing. What she spotted instead was Travis. Though the tiniest flutter rippled through her at the sight of his rugged form striding from the school, she bit down on the inside of her cheek. The man was leaving town. Even if she wanted someone to take her side, Travis wasn't *that* guy.

She fanned Josh's schoolwork. "I expect better from you than this."

"Mo-om. I have to warm up." Josh tried to brush past her.

She moved to block his path. "No, kiddo. What you have to do is listen up. Your grades are more important than baseball. From now on, we have a new rule. For every hour you spend on the ball field, I expect you to spend another hour on your studies. You understand?"

"That's not fair," Josh blustered.

It was her turn to shrug and she put her best effort into it. "Whatever it takes, Josh. You have to do better in school."

Josh tugged his cleats from his backpack. Kicking off his shoes, he threw himself down on the dirt. His harsh "You can't make me" nearly broke her heart.

"Is there a problem?"

At the sound of Travis's voice, Courtney expelled a long breath. She nodded stiffly. "Nothing you need to worry about." She hated the abrupt words but forced herself to hold Travis's gaze while she said them.

Josh stood. In a move that sprayed dirt in all directions, he stubbed his foot into the ground.

"No, Chosh, no!" Addie stomped her feet.

A dark V formed between Travis's brows. Leaning down to pluck the littlest Smith from the ground, the big man cleared his throat. "Josh, I won't tolerate disrespect. You owe your mother an apology."

"Sor-ree." Though the response was immediate, scorn marred the boy's tone. His eyes huge, he pleaded with his coach. "Can't you make her see that practice and games are more important than some stupid old spelling test?"

A lump formed in Courtney's throat. Involving Travis was not where she'd wanted to go. Now, though, she had no choice. She had to make her position clear. She squared her shoulders. "I was explaining that my son has to make his schoolwork a priority."

Dreading Travis's response, she followed his gaze as it slowly drifted to the boy.

"You have a lot of potential," the coach said at last. "I'm not sure if I've ever seen a new player catch on as quickly as you have. I think you could do really well in this sport."

"See, Mom?" Josh crossed his arms.

Courtney let out the breath she'd been holding. Well, what had she expected? That Travis would take her side?

He held up a hand. "But your mom's right. Your studies have to come first. No matter how much I want you to play for the Sluggers, if your grades suffer, you'll be off the team. You got that?"

Courtney blinked. Had she heard correctly? Wondering if her face wore the same blank stare she saw on her son's, she studied Josh. As the realization that he'd lost the battle dawned on him, resignation replaced the defiance he'd carried across his shoulders.

"Yes, Coach," Josh said, his voice subdued. Looking down, he scuffed one foot.

Over his head Courtney mouthed a grateful "Thank you" toward Travis. The shaky smile she aimed at him firmed when he handed Addie to her with a wink and a wide grin.

"Okay, then." Travis lifted one broad shoulder as if he hadn't just knocked her world sideways. "What do you think, Mom? Can Josh practice today or does he need to go home and study?"

Courtney pressed her lips together, certain that if she didn't her mouth would drop wide open. She swept a glance over Travis's impartial expression to study the eager one on Josh's face.

"As long as you get your homework done tonight—" she began.

"I will!" Earnestness beamed from the boy.

"—and study extra hard for your spelling test on Friday, then, yes, you can practice."

Travis clamped a hand on Josh's shoulder. "You're a smart boy. There's no reason why you shouldn't ace all your tests."

As the two of them headed for the field, Courtney shook her head. No doubt about it, she'd misjudged Travis. She'd assumed he was all about baseball. Apparently, he understood the importance of excelling in school, too. Best of all, he wasn't afraid to use his position as coach to bring out the best in her son.

It took a couple of seconds before she could manage more than a whispered "Wow. Didn't see that coming."

Chapter Seven

Travis suppressed a grin as he stepped inside the nearly empty coffee shop. He knew it was wrong to wish he could have Courtney to himself in the mornings. From what he'd gathered, her little café needed all the business it could get. But he couldn't deny how much he enjoyed spending a few quiet moments with her when no one else was around. Three long strides took him to the counter.

"The usual," he said.

Courtney's eyes were such a brilliant blue he thought a man could get lost in them and never regret leaving his map at home. Afraid he might get caught looking, he plucked a five-dollar bill from his wallet and used the excuse to break eye contact.

"We go through this every day." A touch of stubborn independence showed in her gaze. "No charge—"

"And every day I say the same thing," Travis countered. "You can ring up my order. Or I'll simply put the money in the tip jar." He grabbed his coffee and sat at one of the nearby tables where he could watch her work.

"So how's Addie this morning?" he asked while Courtney swept a few crumbs from the counter.

"Still sleeping, thank goodness." More fatigue than

normal showed in her face when she pushed back her hair with one forearm.

"Tough night?"

"She was up and down most of it. I'll be glad when she cuts this new tooth."

He pictured Courtney in a rocking chair, a fussy baby in her arms, and shook his head. His admiration rose as he considered her long days in the shop, followed by even longer nights. Single parenthood was a tough gig.

The bell over the door jingled its reminder that, even on slow days, his time with Courtney never lasted long enough. He sat back while she waited on two new arrivals. When they headed out the door carrying their breakfast orders, he got straight to the point.

"I'm starting Josh in the season opener this weekend." The boys considered it quite the honor to be one of the first nine to take the field.

Courtney's smile faded. "Are you sure he's ready?"

Ready enough that he'd contacted an old friend, suggested he come see the boy. No one judged raw talent better than Frank Booker. The Cannons scout could tell if a kid had potential with just one glimpse.

Sure, Courtney had a thing about baseball, but she'd change her tune if she learned her son was one of those one-in-a-million kids who could go all the way. Who wouldn't? For now, though, there wasn't any sense in raising her hopes—or her dander. He met her gaze.

"We've only practiced for a month, but Josh outplays kids who've been in the majors a year or two. Did he get his talent from you?" The question gave him a darn good excuse to study her compact form.

"Not hardly." She laughed and snapped at him with her dishtowel. "Board games are more my style. I used to work out at the gym but I haven't done that since…" Her laughter died. Staring through the window, she turned somber. "Since Addie was born, I haven't exactly had the time."

Which was just about when she'd lost her husband, according to the school records. Struck by how much responsibility the young widow had shouldered, Travis swigged the last of his coffee. He risked a cautious "Josh's dad, did he play sports?"

"You might say that." Courtney scrubbed the spotless counter.

Her tone carried an uncharacteristic harshness that tasted as bitter as the dregs of his coffee. Though it was nearly time for school, Travis rose for a refill. "You never talk about him," he said softly.

Her hands stilled. She stared down at her ringless fingers. "That's because there's not much to say." A damp, gut-twisting line traced down her cheek. "I knew our marriage was in trouble. He'd grown moody, distant. I thought if we got away—away from his job, from all the tension—we might find our way back to each other." She grabbed a napkin from the dispenser and swiped her nose. "Things didn't turn out like I hoped. By the time I realized they weren't going to, I was already pregnant." She nodded toward her office and the crib where Addie napped.

"So you stayed." A sinking feeling filled his chest at the idea of her trapped in a loveless marriage.

"Yeah, I stayed. I couldn't take his kids from him. Not then. Later, when the truth came out…" Her eyes brimmed. "A car accident took my husband's life, but he'd destroyed our marriage long before that."

More than anything, Travis wanted to wipe away her

tears. She did it first, brushing at them with the back of her hand. At last, she took a breath so deep it made her chest swell. On the slow exhale her posture straightened.

"He cheated, all right? Not just once or twice. A lot."

"What?" His fists tightened. He flexed his hands. Trapped on the other side of the counter, he settled for reaching across it. He cupped Courtney's chin in his fingers, tipping her face up to his. He sought her eyes, captured them with his own and refused to let her look away.

"Courtney," he whispered. "A man would have to be insane or a fool—or both—to cheat on you."

In his hand her chin wobbled.

"Oh, he cheated, all right." A potent mix of emotions swirled in her darkened eyes. "Only, I was too blind to see it. I should have known."

For the first time in his life, Travis wished he were a poet, a wordsmith. He wasn't, but he summoned his best argument.

"He was the blind one for not recognizing what a treasure he had. You deserved better. Look at all you've accomplished." He ran his free hand over the counter. "This café. Your kids. You're a wonderful mom, a smart businesswoman."

As Courtney managed a tremulous smile, he gently released her. His hand dropped to her shoulder, where he traced circles over a few scattered freckles. Though one part of him wished her husband were still alive so he could knock some sense into the idiot, the warm skin beneath his fingers forced him to admit that another part of him was mighty glad Courtney didn't cling to a faded memory.

Why? Because you want her for yourself?

The disturbing truth hit him hard. So hard the jangle of bells announcing the arrival of another customer didn't faze him, because by the time he heard it, he was on his way out the door.

TRAVIS SNUGGED HIS tie into place. He checked his image in the mirror and scowled. A crooked knot would never do. The league president might ignore the dress requirement for him, but was that what he really wanted? He managed not to growl. Breaking the rules—even the little ones—smacked of special treatment. The kind Courtney suspected of all athletes. Resigned to starting over, he loosened the slick silk.

He stopped just long enough to rub the spot in his chest that had ached from the moment she'd told him about her cad of a husband. Ever since, he hadn't been able to get her out of his thoughts. He wanted to prove to her that not all men cheated. That *he* would never.

He was as certain of it as he was that he'd be late for the fund-raiser.

Sure enough, by the time he retraced his route to McLarty Park, cars crowded the parking lot. Music drifted from the rec center, where a DJ spun the latest hits. Travis's strides took him past the front door just as Greg Dowling, president of the Little League, tapped on a microphone. He hustled to join the other coaches, who'd already taken their places at the podium.

"Don't we all clean up nice?" Greg's smile broadened as he gestured to the suit he wore instead of his normal jeans and windbreaker. "You might be used to seeing most of these men in shorts and T-shirts, but there's nothing casual about the way we treat the players on our teams. Every coach here, every parent who spends time in the snack bar, every person involved in Little League wants only the best for today's youth."

A scattering of polite applause erupted. Greg waited for it to die down before he continued.

"Now, you wouldn't be here if you didn't already see the value in what we do. I encourage you all to talk with our coaches, and don't forget to pledge your support."

Greg fanned a handful of forms. Dozens more rested on practically every surface.

"Thanks to a few of our sponsors…"

While the president rattled off the names of several local businesses, Travis's thoughts drifted to one that wasn't included. The league had focused its fund-raising efforts on long-established business owners. Not recent arrivals who, according to the rumor mill, might not be around by the end of the season. He pushed away an image of a closed and shuttered Coffee on Brevard the same way he squashed the picture of a certain upstairs apartment devoid of childish laughter.

Courtney was smart, savvy, driven. She'd make the café work.

Aware that his attention had wandered, he dragged it back in time for Greg's closing remarks.

"There's a cash bar in the corner, just in case a little liquid refreshment will lighten your hold on your wallet." Never one to belabor the point, the president stepped away from the podium while laughter still filled the room.

Free to mingle, Travis spent a few minutes with the manager of a sporting-goods store. While the DJ played one baseball song after another, he congratulated the owner of his favorite Italian restaurant on the man's impending retirement. Making his way through the crowd, he stepped to the closest bar in time to hear ice cubes jostle in an enormous cooler. Three brown bottles clinked as the bartender set beer on the counter.

"Can I buy you a drink?" A reporter from *Florida Today* waved a twenty to catch the bartender's attention. "A beer for me and… What do you want, Coach?"

Travis nodded to the wiry young man behind the bar. "A soda, thanks." Though nothing tasted better than an ice-cold beer after a long day, he still had work to do.

"So, Travis, how do the Sluggers look this year? Think they'll make it all the way this time?"

"To the World Series?" The reporter downed half his bottle with one swig while Travis considered an answer. The man knew as well as he did that trying to predict which team would have a good season and which wouldn't was a wasted effort. There were too many variables. An injury, a few wrong calls. Heck, a key player could come down with the flu and take their chances for tournament play with him. Still, the man had asked.

"You won't be wasting time if you come to a few of our games. Maybe send a photographer."

The reporter grinned as if he'd been given a big scoop. "Will do, Coach."

Whatever he was about to say next died on Travis's lips when he spotted a woman wearing a blue dress that fit her shape as if it had been made for her. He did a double take.

What was she doing here?

"Excuse me," he said, his feet already taking him away from the reporter. He set his soda aside to grab two glasses from a passing tray.

Halfway to her side, he watched Courtney's scan of the room slide to a halt the moment she spotted him. The lips she'd painted a glistening pink curved into a welcoming smile that singled him out. His pace quickened, and he wove past the last of the crowd.

"What a nice surprise." The tiniest flicker of doubt that she was happy to see him faded away when her eyes found his. "Drink?" He held out a ginger ale.

"Thanks." She reached for the glass, her fingers softly brushing his. Her gaze traveled his length. "You make that suit look good."

Glad now that he'd taken the time to redo the knot, Travis smoothed his tie. He swept her with an admiring glance. "You don't look half-bad yourself." He would have said more, but he was afraid he'd come off like a schoolkid with his first crush. In truth, Courtney looked so ravishing his fingers literally ached with the need to slide around her waist and pull her close. His gaze skimmed over fabric that fell from her shoulders to a tantalizing neckline. A low-slung belt hugged her slim hips. He followed the skirt that swirled above her knees to barely caress her shapely calves. His focus dropped lower, to shoes that were all thin straps with the sweetest little bows at the toes.

He shot the cuff of one sleeve and tightened his grip on his soda while he searched for an innocuous topic.

"Where are the kids?"

"With a babysitter. Melinda and I are splitting the cost." She sipped her drink, her lips leaving the tiniest pink smudge on the rim of the glass. "She and her husband insisted I come with them. I hope it's okay."

"Better than okay," he said, his voice low. "I have to talk to some people, but I'd welcome the company if you're game."

"That sounds like a lot more fun than standing here by myself."

"Oh, I don't think you'd be alone for very long." He gave her a teasing grin. There was practically no chance of the prettiest girl in the room turning into a wallflower. Why, if he walked away, guys would line up to sweep her off her feet. He scoured the room. There weren't many singles at the event, but he wouldn't put it past one or two wolves to make a move. Feeling a little possessive, he held out his arm. His chest swelled when Courtney threaded her fingers through his.

The next hour flew by. At the end of it, Travis had spoken with every business owner in attendance, obtained the desired support from most of them and thanked each one profusely for helping out. He was just slipping the final pledge card into his pocket when the DJ ran out of songs about baseball. The soulful opening notes of "Lay Down Beside Me" drifted from the giant speakers. Glancing down at the woman who'd spent time making small talk with people she barely knew, he convinced himself she deserved to relax a bit.

"Would you like to take a spin?" He held his breath while he waited for an answer that seemed as important as throwing a perfect strike.

His heart thudded faster when Courtney stared up at him, indecision playing across her face.

"It's only a dance," he whispered, trying without much luck to put them both at ease.

"Why not?" She nodded at last.

His hand at the small of her back, he steered her toward a clear space before either of them changed their minds. He told himself a single dance didn't mean anything, but the minute he slipped his arm around Courtney's waist, Travis knew he was lost. As he took her in his arms, her head rested perfectly below his shoulder. When she leaned into him, it felt so right that he never wanted to let her go. Enveloped by her spicy floral scent, he drank it in, unable to get enough of it. Of her.

For the first time since the day the slender blonde had walked into Bob Morgan's office, Travis couldn't think of one good reason why they shouldn't explore their feelings. The children were no longer the stumbling blocks he'd thought they'd be. Addie already had him wrapped around her little finger. As for Josh, he was a great kid on his way to becoming a better one. And while Courtney might never enjoy baseball, she'd shoved her own doubts and concerns aside to help her son.

He bent so low that her hair tickled his chin. It stirred an urge to brush a kiss through the soft strands. He indulged himself, only to realize it wasn't enough. He wanted—no, he needed—he needed to feel the press of her lips on his. If for no other reason than to know whether she felt the same way.

He whisked her through the open doors and onto the porch, where volunteers had strung twinkling strands among the ivy. Earlier he hadn't seen the point of all the decorations. Now the lights shone for Courtney, and she'd never looked more beautiful.

She peered up at him, laughter dancing across the lips he meant to claim. As he met her gaze and held it, an altogether different emotion darkened her blue eyes. When she shifted marginally closer, Travis suppressed a moan.

"Courtney, I—" His voice failed him.

"Yeah, I know."

Her fingers trailed across his jaw. He captured them in his hand and pressed a kiss into her palm.

"Whatever this is, I don't think I can fight it anymore."

He didn't wait for her response. Instead, he slowly lowered his head until his lips met the smooth skin above her eyebrows. He swept across it, barely making contact. Hunger roared within him to have more of her, but he forced himself to go slow, to give her time to back away if she wanted.

She didn't resist. He dipped lower. And lower still. Finally reaching her lips, he rained tiny kisses across them.

Was that his imagination, or had she kissed him back?

Taking a chance, he pressed more firmly. Her soft sigh let him know he was on the right track and he angled closer, reveling in the heady sensations that her touch sent through his body. Unable, unwilling, to stop himself, he swept his tongue against her mouth. She opened to him, and the move sent a surge of pure pleasure down his spine.

Travis smiled without breaking contact. She tasted sweet with a hint of flowers and spice. He threaded one hand through her hair. The other, he slipped around her waist, drawing her to him until his legs pressed against hers. He melted into her as music drifted through the open doorway and lights twinkled among the vines overhead.

He could have gone on for hours, lost in that one kiss. Would have…if the song hadn't ended. But the moment the DJ's booming voice announced the next number, Courtney broke away. Abruptly, she stepped out of his embrace.

"I— We— I can't," she said, breathless.

In an instant, she had slipped through the doors and disappeared into the crowded room.

He watched her go without making a move to stop

her. He understood. Or at least, he thought he did. He ran a hand through hair she had disheveled, blotted her lipstick from his lips. Discovering he had fallen for her had hit him so hard he couldn't blame her for running. For cutting things off in the middle of the most incredible kiss he'd ever experienced.

He could hardly wait for the next one but told himself there was no need to hurry. Tomorrow was the start of the Little League baseball season. They had six weeks or more to get to know each other better. Determined to use the time to learn all he could about Courtney and her children, he turned toward the parking lot and headed for home.

HEAVEN HELP HER.

When Travis's lips had brushed hers, it was as if someone had thrown a switch. Her heavy burdens had slipped from her shoulders. The worries that kept her up most nights had melted away. His touch had ignited a rush of wondrous sensations she hadn't felt in longer than she d remember. For a few minutes, she'd lost herself in his caresses, his heady blend of desire and strength. She'd wished those feelings could last forever.

But no sooner had Melinda and the babysitter toted the sleepy Markham children down the stairs than reality came rushing back to confront her.

Her life was in shambles because of a baseball player. No matter how different Travis was from her late husband, his life was still devoted to the sport that had destroyed her marriage. Worse, at his first chance to coach in the pros, Travis would leave town. While her children, her life, remained in Cocoa Village.

She stared at a thin crack in the plaster ceiling. As attracted as she was to Travis, there'd be no more kissing. No more long, lingering looks. No wishing for a second chance at love. Friendship—that was all she could afford to give him. Friendship and nothing more.

Could she do it? Could she back away from Travis?

For her children, for her own sanity, she didn't have a choice. Calling a halt to whatever this was between them wouldn't be easy. From the way Travis had whispered her name as his fingers skimmed over her bare shoulders, she knew he was drawn to her. But pursuing a relationship when they couldn't have a future together made no sense.

With that thought, she punched her pillows, closed her eyes and willed herself to lie still, even if sleep was impossible. It wouldn't do to show up at the ball field with dark circles under her eyes, fatigue written on her face. Not the way a certain hunky coach paid attention to details.

"Six weeks," she whispered on her way to the opening-day ceremony the next morning. "Just six weeks."

She could smile and guard her heart against Travis that long. In less than two months, she'd have fulfilled her part of the bargain she'd made with Principal Morgan. Once she'd secured her son's place at school, she'd never see Travis for coffee in the morning, never look into his bedroom eyes, never be alone with him and in danger of succumbing to his kisses again.

Six weeks. She could stay strong that long, couldn't she?

She had to.

At McLarty Park, "Put Me In, Coach" blared from the score booth. One by one, teams of young players marched onto the field. Their jerseys created a brilliant kaleidoscope above blindingly white pants. From her seat in the bleachers, Courtney spotted Josh, standing a half head taller than his teammates. She smiled and waved, determined not to let her decision about Travis spoil her son's big day.

Bouncing Addie on her lap, she pointed. "See Josh, honey? Wave to him."

"Chosh! Chosh!"

The little girl struggled to climb out of her lap, but Courtney made a game of hugging her daughter close. This wasn't a practice, where she and the other moms could rely on one another to look out for their youngsters. Today hundreds of parents, assorted relatives and complete strangers filled the stadium. Letting her baby out of her grasp wasn't an option.

She ducked as Addie's arms flailed the air. The baby ratcheted up the volume. "Cosh Oak!" she squealed. "Cosh Oak!"

Courtney braced herself for the disappointed wails that would surely come when Travis turned his back on her child. Not that she blamed him. He was, after all, in the middle of a ball field. Not the ideal place to play with a toddler.

How he managed to pick her daughter's voice out of the din, Courtney didn't know, but somehow Travis did. His stride across the field to his team broke. She stared, disbelief sending a flutter through her when he made a show of catching Addie's imaginary kiss. He slipped the *treasure* in his pants pocket and gave the baby a jaunty wave before he rejoined his team.

The sensation of being in Travis's arms flooded back. Her tummy tightened, and Courtney stifled a groan. In the wee hours of the morning, her plan to stay away from the coach had made perfect sense. But getting through an entire baseball season without giving her heart to the man would be harder than she'd thought.

Soon after the teams marched out of the stadium, the crowd thinned. Over the loudspeakers, an announcer encouraged the few lingerers to clear the field for the start of the season's first game, pitting the Hornets versus the Sluggers. Off to one side, Courtney glimpsed Travis leading his team through their pregame warm-ups. A short time later the umpire called, "Play ball!"

Fighting an urge to bite her fingernails, Courtney plastered on a bright smile. Inside, though, her body thrummed with a nervousness she'd never felt in a major league park. When Josh trotted onto the infield, she scooted forward. By the time Tommy Markham threw the first pitch, she literally sat on the edge of her seat.

For two innings neither team scored a run. But at the top of the third, the Hornets managed to get runners on all the bases before the end of the inning. With an out remaining, the opposing coach signaled for a substitute.

Unease rippled through the Sluggers' stands when a big kid, easily twenty pounds heavier than anyone on their team, lumbered out of the dugout. In the batter's box, he hit his bat against his cleats. *Thud, thud, thud.* The noise echoed through the silent bleachers.

On the mound, Tommy's face bore a decidedly worried look. Courtney risked a single glimpse at Travis, but if the coach was concerned, he hid it well. Taking her cue from him, she summoned some encouragement.

"You can do it, Sluggers!" she cheered.

The batter shifted his weight, settling in over the plate as if he owned it.

Tommy went into his windup.

Courtney held her breath. Her stomach churned. "Oh, please," she whispered. *Please what? Please let Tommy throw a strike? Please let us get out of this inning? Please let us win the game?* Surprised by how much she wanted the latter, she braced for the pitch.

Thwack!

The ball sailed off the end of the bat. A high pop-up, it drifted down toward Josh. He reached up, neatly trapping the white leather in the glove Travis had given him. Stunned, Courtney added her own cheers to those of the rest of the parents as Josh ran toward the dugout with his teammates.

Play resumed, but the Hornets had lost their momentum and the Sluggers easily won. Afterward the players and their coach lined up at home plate, where they shook the hands of their opponents before they walked off the field. Now that the game had ended, Courtney felt a sudden need to put some distance between herself and all things baseball. Especially a certain tall, handsome coach. One who personified sportsmanship during the game, not even raising his voice when things looked particularly bad.

If Josh *had* to play baseball, he was lucky to have Travis for his coach.

Even if she didn't want him for herself.

Much.

"Great game!" she exclaimed later as she helped Josh load his gear into the trunk.

"Did you see my catch, Mom? I didn't get a hit, but Coach Oak said that's okay. He said the other team gave up after I caught the ball, and one player can't do everything." Excitement and little-boy sweat filled the car when the boy slid onto the seat beside Addie. "We're s'posed to follow everyone else. Coach Oak is taking the whole team for pizza. The guys said he does every Saturday. There he goes." Josh jabbed a finger toward Travis's Jeep. "Let's go. I don't want to be late. Tommy said I could sit beside him."

"Really?" Courtney tugged her Sluggers baseball cap from her head and tossed it onto the passenger seat. "I don't know."

"We have to go, Mom! The whole team will be there."

She studied her son's eager face in the rearview mirror, drew in a fortifying breath and started the car. She pulled in behind the line that followed Travis's Jeep to a family-owned restaurant. Walking past festive banners and helium balloons that wished someone a bon voyage, Courtney told herself it wasn't as if she and the coach would be spending time alone. They'd be surrounded by parents and other players. In a group that size, surely she could keep her distance.

Or not.

She gritted her teeth when Melinda waved her toward a seat she'd saved next to the one man Courtney wanted to avoid.

"I need a high chair for Addie." Courtney eyed tables that had been pushed together and covered with red-checked vinyl. Players at one end, coaches and parents at the other, people sat elbow to elbow.

"No problem. I'll get it."

Before she could protest, Travis disappeared. He returned minutes later with a high chair, which he placed next to his spot at the table.

"Here you go, Addie." He plucked the all-too-willing baby from Courtney's arms and plopped her onto the seat.

Courtney watched in amazement as the coach deftly belted Addie in.

"I ordered bread sticks." Travis's grin tilted dangerously. "And ketchup." He rubbed Addie's head. "I hope that's okay."

More than okay, it was perfect. *He* was perfect.

Her hard-won determination to maintain a safe distance from Travis shuddered as Courtney slid into the chair next to his. She glanced around the room. Her daughter looked up at Travis with adoring eyes. At the other end of the table, Josh thought the coach walked on water.

And she, what did she think?

She thought she should have been paying better attention because, while she wasn't looking, Travis had stolen a piece of her heart.

Chapter Eight

Travis slowed, his thoughts spinning like a well-thrown curve. He should stop. Turn around. Get in his car and drive home, to school, to a batting cage. Go anywhere but Coffee on Brevard. There was too much at stake for him to take things with Courtney beyond a few stolen kisses—a few stolen *amazing* kisses. Not unless they were in it for the long haul. Unless *he* was in it for the long haul.

Was that what he wanted? Did he want to have it all with Courtney? The house, the white picket fence, the two—maybe three—children playing in the backyard?

Josh and Addie didn't deserve an *Uncle* Travis in their lives. A man who stopped by between road trips. No, they needed a real dad. Someone who would teach Josh how to handle long division and throw a slider. Who wasn't afraid to play dolls with Addie but would put the fear of God into anyone who tried to hurt her.

Was he willing to be that man? To settle for teaching school and coaching Little League for the rest of his life?

For the first time ever, saying no to the Cannons didn't feel like settling. It felt right.

Stunned by the insight, Travis came to a dead stop in

the middle of the sidewalk. He stared at gulls that flew so low over the river their wings nearly skimmed the water.

He gulped, his shoulders squaring.

Let's not be too hasty here, he told himself.

He and Courtney had a long way to go before he considered giving up his dream job. They still had a lot to learn about each other. And then there was her dislike of all things baseball. There was still room for improvement on that score. He crossed his fingers, hoping the trip to Twister Stadium would erase her final reservations about the sport that defined his life.

He put his feet in motion again. The bell over the door jingled as he stepped into the café. His stomach protested its current empty state the moment he sniffed a delicious mix of coffee and fresh cinnamon buns. He scanned empty tables and Courtney's vacant spot behind the counter.

Where was she?

He wove through the café until he spotted a dead-to-the-world Addie sprawled in her Pack 'n Play. When she was awake, she kept them all on their toes. Knowing the tyke had put a goofy smile on his lips and not caring, he poked his head through the open doorway of Courtney's office.

"Mornin'," he called. "Where is everybody?"

Her head swiveled up from her computer screen, the deep V between her brows thinning when she smiled.

"You missed the rush when I opened the doors. A big cruise ship docked overnight in Port Canaveral. Today it'll offer an excursion to quaint Cocoa Village, so most of the shops will be open, even though it's Monday."

"Is that why there's enough sweets in the display case to give the entire town a sugar high?" He noted the fatigue lines around Courtney's mouth and wondered how late she'd worked last night or how early she'd had to start baking. He summoned a supportive smile. "That must be good for business."

"Yes, but…" With a soft sigh, she tilted away from her desk. "Don't get me wrong, I'm happy for the sales, but these people are only here for a couple of hours before they go back aboard and disappear. What would really help are some long-term repeat customers." She cast a worried look at the computer screen.

"Everything all right?" he asked, eyeing neatly organized piles of bills and receipts.

"Not exactly." This time her sigh came out as a low whistle. "You ever see that old cartoon with the guy in the leaky rowboat? The one where he's trying to bail with a slotted spoon? That's me."

Her voice carried an ominous ring he didn't like. "Business not going well?"

"That's an understatement. Most days, it costs more to keep the doors open than I bring in." She tucked a loose curl behind her ear.

Travis considered all that Coffee on Brevard had to offer—the perfect location, food like his mama wished she could make, great coffee.

"Just hang in there," he offered. "Once people discover the café, they'll come back again and again." Trying to lighten the mood, he grinned and pointed to himself. "Like I have."

But Courtney only shook her head. "It's spring. The winter residents that are the mainstay of every restaurant and bar in the county—they're packing up and heading north. From what the other shop owners tell me, Cocoa

Village is a ghost town through most of the summer. I'm not sure I can keep going till next fall."

"What would you do instead?" With a start, he realized how little he knew about her background.

She shrugged. "I'd hate to uproot the kids again, especially Josh. He's really turning a corner. But none of my options are all that great." She tapped a pencil against the edge of the desk. "We could go to my dad's in Arizona, I guess. Until I get back on my feet again."

At the thought of not stopping by Coffee on Brevard for his morning fix of Courtney and caffeine, a knife-like pain sliced through Travis's gut. He clutched the doorjamb, steadying himself, while reality sank a little deeper. Somewhere along the way, he'd completely fallen for the young widow and her family. So much so that before he'd walked through her door, he'd considered settling down just to be with them.

But they might move away? Though he wasn't sure he'd like the answer, he asked when she'd have to decide.

Her pencil picked up the tempo. "I can make it through the end of the school year. Not much longer."

Travis mopped his face. Ed, the owner of the Italian restaurant where the team usually celebrated, had decided to throw down the dough and retire. Which meant the Sluggers needed a new place for their after-game parties. He tilted his head to the side.

"Are there rules about what you can or can't serve?" He pointed toward the empty tables.

Courtney's eyebrows hiked. "I don't have a liquor license, if that's what you mean."

He let his words slow. "You know the place where we ate Saturday? It sold. The new owners are turning it into a tapas bar."

"Yeah?" Courtney's face filled with questions.

"What if, after Ed's changes hands, *you* hosted the team's next party? I could—I don't know—pick up pizzas somewhere. Or have them delivered," he said, making up a plan as he went along. "The parents could do the same thing. You could supply the drinks. Maybe some desserts. I know you wouldn't make any money. Or at least not much. But, well, it might lead to something."

His shoulders slumped. It wasn't the brightest idea he'd ever had. But he had to face it—desperate times called for desperate measures.

"You know I have a brick oven, don't you?"

Not certain why that mattered, he scratched his head.

"It makes the most marvelous pizzas. When I offer them as the lunch special, I always sell out. It wouldn't be all that hard to make enough for the team…and everyone else." Her words came more quickly as she eyed the seating area. "I'd need more tables and chairs. Maybe those long narrow ones like they have in the rec center. And some tablecloths, but they're cheap. I'd keep the menu simple to start. Maybe just pepperoni or cheese. Salad. Soda wouldn't be any problem. I already stock that."

Watching Courtney turn his idea into an honest-to-goodness plan warmed the cold that had spread through his chest. "I can borrow the tables and chairs. You just tell me how many you need. I'll bring them over in the Jeep."

"This could work, Travis. It could be just the thing I needed to stir up new business."

A heady excitement hummed through the room. Courtney rose from her desk and flew into his arms. "Travis, this is such a great idea. I don't know how to thank you."

He peered down at the pert features where happiness had set up shop. The possible ways she could thank him were endless, but he had one in particular in mind. He dropped a tiny kiss on the tip of her upturned nose.

"Well, you can help me with the end-of-the-season trip to Twister Stadium. We need to start planning it."

As suddenly as Courtney had filled his arms, she emptied them. "That's not for, what—five more weeks?" She leaned against her desk, her features tightening. "I told you I wasn't going."

Travis held up his hands. "Hey, I'm a pretty big guy, but there's no way the assistant coach and I can manage twelve boys at the stadium by ourselves. The team mom always comes along to help out."

Determination settled onto Courtney's face. "Sorry. You'll need to get someone else."

He thought back to the day they'd gone over the team-mom duties. She hadn't seemed happy about the prospect of a trip to Twister Stadium then, but he'd shrugged aside her concerns, certain she'd get over them. Apparently she hadn't. It was time to pull out his most persuasive arguments.

"The league's insurance only covers the coaches and the team mom. That's you. If you back out, I'll have to cancel. You don't want to do that to the boys, do you? Besides, didn't you just say you owed me? Do this, and we'll call it even."

He had her there and they both knew it. Courtney looked as though she'd just swallowed a dose of bitter medicine when she said, "All right," through clenched teeth.

There was a story behind her reluctance and Travis was determined to uncover it, but the doorbell at the entrance to the café tinkled, silencing his questions. A group of chattering tourists buzzed into the dining area. Courtney immediately shifted into business mode.

"We'll talk more later," she said, edging past him without the hoped-for kiss.

Puzzled by Courtney's reaction, he nodded to the tourists on his way out the door. He was halfway to his car before he remembered that he hadn't so much as snagged himself a sweet roll.

"Josh, you have your baseball glove?" Courtney stuffed a fresh pack of baby wipes into Addie's diaper bag.

"Got it." He ran down the list. "Hat. Glove. Cleats. Batting glove. Bat. Water bottle." His lopsided grin warned of an impending joke. He pointed down. "Cup. Can we go now?"

"Thanks for the picture, mister." The child who was growing up before she was ready shifted his weight from one leg to the other at the door. "Cool your jets. We have plenty of time. Besides, we need to talk. I got a phone call from your teacher yesterday."

Josh's teasing grin froze. "I've been doing better at school, Mom. Honest."

"That's exactly what Ms. Culpepper said." Courtney dropped the diaper bag at Josh's feet. "I just wanted to tell you how proud I am of you." Seeing him standing there in his Sluggers uniform, she couldn't deny how much he'd changed, thanks in large part to Travis and the extra time he'd spent with her son. The bitter, angry young boy had all but disappeared. In his place stood the one she remembered from better days.

Josh stepped back as she reached for him. "Thanks, Mom. But I'm too old for that."

"Since when?" Over his good-natured protests, she wrapped her arms around his shoulders. "You'll never be too old for one of your mama's hugs."

"Okay, okay." Josh tolerated the embrace for all of two seconds before ducking out of it. "Can we goooo noooowww?" he begged.

"The game doesn't start till noon. What's the hurry?"

An earnest expression sharpened his features. "Coach Oak said I'm pitching today. I want to get there early and warm up."

"Ever think you should share that news with your mom?" Courtney threaded her ponytail through the back of a Sluggers ball cap. Butterflies filled her tummy when she thought of all the responsibility that rested on a pitcher's shoulders. She took a calming breath.

"Didn't I just tell you?" Josh eyed her quizzically.

"Never mind." Destroying the boy's confidence before his first appearance on the mound was so *not* what she wanted to do. "Let me just round up your sister." She headed down the short hall. "Addie," she called. "Let's go."

At McLarty Park, red clay and white chalk glistened beneath the midmorning sun.

"There's Coach." Josh pointed toward Travis leaning against the fence at Field Number One, where another game was underway.

Doubt ate at Courtney when the excitement level in the car kicked up a notch. Was she making the second-biggest mistake in her life by letting her children get close to Travis? The whole family had developed quite the case of hero worship for the man who'd made a habit of stopping by Coffee on Brevard every weekday morning. He'd turned out to be the kind of stable, trustworthy man she wanted for her son's role model. He treated Addie like a princess. He'd even come up with an idea that might keep her business afloat.

But he was leaving town. Headed for a job in the sport that had stolen her children's father from them. One part of her said she should cut her ties to Travis now, before things went too far. The other part argued that it was already too late.

She wrenched her thoughts back where they belonged when the car door sprang open.

"Bye, Mom!" Without being reminded, Josh grabbed Addie's diaper bag along with his gear. He dropped the pink tote at Courtney's usual spot beneath the trees on his way to his coach.

While the boys hit the batting cages before the rest of the team arrived, Courtney spread a blanket beneath the shade tree. She gathered Addie into her lap. They'd giggled their way through a third reading of *Are You My Mother?* by the time Melinda Markham unfolded a chair at the edge of the blanket.

"How's our pitcher's *mom* this morning? Are you *nervous?*"

"More than I thought I'd be." A faint tremble shook Courtney's hand as she handed Addie juice in a sippy cup. Done with her books, the little girl scrambled down from Courtney's lap.

"Mom, I gotta go." The carrot-topped youth at Melinda's side stamped his feet.

"Hey, Tommy. How's the arm?" Courtney gave the pitcher the standard greeting.

"Oh, he's fine." Melinda spoke for her son. Turning to him, she continued, "Now, go root for Josh. If we get into a hole, it'll be up to you to dig us out when Coach brings you in to replace him."

A chill crept up Courtney's back despite the balmy breeze that sent a palm frond skittering along the left-field fence. She quashed the fleeting thought that Melinda might be right, that her son wasn't ready for such a huge challenge, that the team could lose because of him.

One glimpse of Travis stepping from behind the dug-out banished her fears. The man's confidence showed in every step he took. From home plate he gave Josh the thumbs-up sign before the coach donned a thick protective vest and catcher's mask. When her heart thudded in her chest, Courtney knew Travis, not Josh, had caused it.

She squinted until her vision shrank to a thin slit. She held her breath as Josh went into his windup. A fastball barreled through the strike zone and smacked into Travis's glove.

"Good one," Travis called.

In a move that captured the attention of every woman within sight and sent Courtney's pulse into overdrive, the coach rose to a half crouch. Muscles flexing, he fired the ball to Josh before sinking into the catcher's position again.

"Wow. He's really improved since tryouts."

Courtney focused on her son. Josh had changed a lot in the weeks since the draft.

Was it enough?

She tapped fingers against her chair's plastic armrest when the umpire called, "Play ball!" To her relief, Josh threw consistent heat straight across the plate. One after another, their opponent's batters struck out and retired to the dugout. After four innings, the Sluggers were well ahead when Travis wandered over to the backstop. He looped his fingers through the chain link.

"I'm pulling Josh out now," he said, aiming his remarks at Courtney. "He's done a great job, but he's thrown ninety pitches. That's enough for an unseasoned player."

More familiar with the importance of pitch counts than anyone knew, she only nodded.

"He did better than I expected." Melinda's mouth gaped open as the coach walked away. Her focus wandered. "I wonder why he didn't put Tommy in," she said, scowling at the sixth grader who'd replaced Josh on the mound.

"This game is practically in the bag," Courtney offered. Ahead by eight runs, the Sluggers needed only two more to invoke the mercy clause and go home with another win in their pockets. "I bet Coach is saving Tommy for the next time. No sense risking his arm when there's no need."

"What are you trying to do? Ruin my son's chances?" The harsh whisper sliced through the air.

"Wh-what?" Courtney stammered. She shrank into her chair.

Though they were far from the bleachers where most of the parents sat, Melinda leaned in close. "You're too new to realize it, but the slightest hint of an injury can ruin a player's chances to turn pro."

Wrong on all counts.

Courtney suppressed a laugh. She probably knew more about baseball than anyone on the field, including Travis. She could write a book about the aches, the pains, the sprains every player in the league suffered. As for Melinda's son...

"You think Tommy—" she started slowly.

"I'm sure of it." Melinda flopped back. "So is Coach. That's why he wanted my Tommy on his team." She frowned, then added, "And Josh. Playing for the Sluggers gives the boy—gives both our boys—a chance to prove they have what it takes. Coach Oak will spread the word. Scouts will get the message and come look at them. It's how our sons will make it to the next level."

Courtney ran her fingers through her ponytail. Snagging one of only twelve hundred spots on the major league rosters took more than the recommendation of a Little League coach. It took physical ability and talent, loads of it. Not to mention luck. None of which was under the players'—or their coach's—control.

"At this age, our boys should play sports because they enjoy it," she said, surprised at how much her opinion had changed in just eight weeks.

"Oh, no." Melinda shook her head. "We need to pull out all the stops *now* if they're ever going to have a chance. Why, Tom practices with Tommy every night. They're already working on his curveball. We have a batting cage and a pitching machine in our backyard, and we're enrolling Tommy in an exclusive baseball camp on the West Coast."

Courtney held up a hand. "That's a lot of pressure to put on a boy who hasn't even finished elementary school, don't you think?" She shuddered to imagine how her friend would react the first time her son got cut from a team. Or worse, bombed out of tryouts. She'd seen firsthand the damage such single-mindedness could do.

And with a sigh, she realized she didn't know whether Travis shared Melinda's opinion or not.

Meeting Josh at the car minutes after the game, she

ran a hand through his tousled hair and gave her son a
heartfelt "You looked good out there."

He grinned up at her. "Bobby Jones wants me to ride
with him to get pizza. Can I, Mom?"

No sooner did the words tumble from his mouth
than an oversize SUV slowed to a stop at Courtney's
bumper. The passenger-side window glided down, and
Betty Jones motioned. "Come on, Josh. We have plenty
of room."

The chance to hash things out with Travis while the
team headed for the pizza party was too good to pass
up. Courtney waited all of two seconds before giving
her permission. She retrieved Addie's car seat from the
back of the sedan. With her little girl toddling along at
her side, she headed for the coach's Jeep while second
thoughts crowded her mind.

What if Travis shared Melinda's insistence that everything in a young boy's life should revolve around
baseball? Her heart hammered when she considered the
possible outcome of their talk. And with a start, the truth
hit home.

As much as she fought it, as often as she reminded
herself that the man wasn't going to stick around, each
day brought her a little closer to falling for Travis.

Yet she had to ask the tough questions. Had to know if
there was room in his heart for more than a round white
ball and a leather glove. Her arms crossed, she stiffened
her spine and her determination to learn the truth about
the coach.

Addie had no such qualms. She held out her arms to
Travis as soon as he got within reach.

"Hey, Addie," he cooed to the baby. "How's my little

girl today? You going to ride with me?" He pointed toward the car seat at Courtney's feet.

"If that's all right." She forced the words through
trembling lips.

Addie tugged at Travis's baseball cap until she held
it in her chubby hands. With hardly any effort at all,
he lifted the toddler high in the air. "Where's your big
brother, huh?"

Her voice shaky, Courtney told him Josh had gone
ahead. "They'll meet us at the restaurant." Now that
the moment was upon her, she had trouble forming the
words. "Travis, we…um…we need to talk."

Talk, the four letters that spelled sayonara, adios,
goodbye. The unexpected word rocked Travis to his
cleats.

One look at Courtney's pale face and rigid posture
told him something had gone horribly wrong. Feeling
as though he'd just been slammed in the gut, he lowered
Addie to the ground.

"Talk, huh?"

Buying time, he stowed his gear in the back of the
Jeep and lowered the hatch.

"Hop in, then." He pretended the installation of the
baby's car seat required his full concentration while he
used the time to pull the torn edges of his composure
together. Once everyone was buckled in, he sped past
Ed's Italian, where banners announced the restaurant's
final weekend.

"Where are we going?" Courtney broke the silence.

His voice rough, he answered, "Thought we'd find
someplace quiet since you wanted to—" he expelled a
breath "—talk. I don't know about you, but I don't want

the whole team hanging on every word." He shrugged. "No one will mind if we're a little late."

He slowed onto a winding, twisty road under a canopy of towering oaks. At a grassy spot overlooking the wide river he pulled onto the shoulder. The windows down, he swiveled to check on the baby in the backseat.

Addie's head lolled to one side, a tiny bubble of drool on her lips. His chest tightened when he considered that, depending on how the conversation went, he might not play a part in the little girl's life. He barely gathered enough spit to swallow before he turned to face the woman he was crazy about.

His tongue stuck to the roof of his mouth. He pried it loose. "So…" he began.

Courtney studied him, her eyes filled with questions. "Why didn't you put Tommy in to pitch today?"

"Tommy?" Of all the scenarios that had been running through his head, none of them started with one of his players. "That's what you brought me out here for?"

A frown niggled Courtney's lips. "Yes," she said slowly. "What'd you think?"

"Oh, I don't know." Travis ran a hand through sweat-dampened hair. "Usually, when a woman says she wants to talk, she means it's over. Which is kind of crazy since we barely know one another. But I was hoping we at least had a chance…" His voice trailed off.

Courtney's eyes widened. "I…uh…I really wanted to talk about the Markhams."

The bands constricting his chest eased the tiniest bit. A long relief-filled breath seeped through his lips. He thought back to the game and did his best to answer her question.

"About Tommy. The boy already threw twice this

week. We've got some tough competition coming up. I thought it'd be better to rest him for a couple of days." He clutched the steering wheel and stared out over the river. Halfway through the season, the Sluggers had won every game.

"Melinda says you want your players to concentrate solely on baseball. Nothing else. She's convinced Tommy will play pro ball and that you're on board with that." She seemed to think better of what she'd said and gave a nervous laugh. "Oh, what do I know."

"Whoa, now!" Travis held up a finger. "You know me better than that."

"That's just the problem. I don't." Courtney let out a thready breath and met his gaze. "I want to, though. I—I guess it's time we talk about why I have such a hard time with Josh playing baseball."

He'd known all along there was more to her story than a simple dislike of the sport. No one took such a vehement stand without a reason. Glad she finally trusted him enough to share hers, he settled back, waiting for her to continue. But Courtney fell silent for so long that at last he prompted her. "This is obviously a touchy subject. Did something happen to you?"

"My husband. My late husband." Her face crumpled. For one brief moment, her shoulders rounded. Then, just as Travis decided to take her in his arms and tell her he didn't need to hear any more if it was too hard for her, she straightened.

"He cheated—you knew that. That wasn't the worst of it."

Not the worst? Travis noted the slight hitch in her voice. What else had she been through?

"From the moment he, uh, he landed his first job, that

became Priority Number One. He had to be the best.
Earn the biggest salary. Have the most toys. He turned
being a workaholic into such an art form that I never
questioned the late nights, the weekends he traveled—"
she made air quotes "—on business. If he had a bad day
or a bad week, he took his frustrations out on everyone.
Me. Josh."

Now that she'd started, her words tumbled out in a
rush. "He never actually struck us. No matter what, I'd
have left if he did. But he was driven. Had to have a fancier car. A bigger house. Hold his liquor better and, as it
turned out, have more women. Before I knew how bad
things had gotten, the police were at the door. They said
he'd wrapped his car around a tree. He died at the scene.
His date was luckier. She only spent the next month in
the hospital."

Travis sucked in a breath. "I had no idea." His arms
literally ached to reach out to her, but she'd wedged herself into the far corner. He wondered if she realized she'd
crossed her arms as if she was trying to protect herself.

"That crash took everything I had, except for the
kids." She stared out the window, refusing to meet his
eyes. "Right after the funeral, I found out he'd blown
through every dime of our savings—all to impress the
latest in a long string of other women. The one with
him that night, she sued. The settlement took the little
we had left."

She sighed. "Of course, I was the last to know. His
bosses. His te— His coworkers. Their wives. They'd all
kept his secrets."

He sensed she was only skimming the surface, that
there were other, more hurtful truths she wasn't ready to
tell him. He swallowed. If he'd known what she'd been

through that first day in Bob's office, he'd have gone easier on her.

"So you packed up the kids and moved here?" he asked when she didn't say anything more.

Courtney nodded. "I salvaged what little I could before the creditors took over. It was enough to open the café. Barely."

Travis's heart ached for the tears that dripped down her cheeks when she turned to face him.

"I like you," she admitted, her voice a breathy whisper. "I think you like me, too."

"More than you know." Reaching out, he stroked her forearm. She trembled but didn't resist when he took her hand in his.

"Travis, I…I need to know how you feel about this thing with Tommy. I've been down that road. I know where such single-mindedness can lead. I need to know you do, too."

Travis's hand stilled. She wasn't the only one with secrets.

"Did I ever tell you why I don't play baseball anymore?

Courtney's eyes narrowed. "You got cut, didn't you?"

"That's what most people think. The real story isn't the kind of thing players bandy about in the locker rooms." Only a handful of people knew the whole truth, and suddenly, he wanted Courtney to be one of them.

"I was this close to making it to the Show." He pressed his forefinger to his thumb until they nearly touched. "The Cannons' ace had torn a rotator cuff. Their bull pen was struggling and it was just a matter of time before they called me up. That day, in Saint Louis, a scout I knew was in the stands. I had to make a good impression, so I put everything I had into the ball. I threw harder, faster, than I ever had…and wound up cracking three ribs in the process."

She sucked in a gasp. "Oh, Travis. I'm so sorry."

He glanced over at her. So much pain and sympathy swam in her eyes that he'd have sworn she knew the injury was a career ender. Which was ridiculous considering her aversion to sports.

"I had to make a choice. I could lie, load up on pain pills and continue to pitch. Or quit. It was touch and go there for a little while." The time he spent struggling with the decision wasn't his proudest moment. "In the end, I chose to walk away. It was either that or hurt myself and the game I love."

Understanding flickered in Courtney's blue eyes. Without thinking about it, he pulled her into his arms. The need to feel her lips on his, to sweep her into his heart, took control and for a while he lost himself in the touch of her hands on his skin, the feel of her beneath his fingers.

They were both slightly breathless by the time Addie's giggles rose from the backseat.

Reluctantly, Travis brushed his lips against Courtney's upturned nose. He smiled as she smoothed her loose curls. He loved the way his kisses turned her lips rosy and put a hitch in her breath. He wanted to see where things were headed but reminded himself that with Courtney it had to be all about the small steps. Content that the one they'd just taken made the future look a whole lot brighter than it had a half hour earlier, he started the car and headed back the way they'd come.

Chapter Nine

Courtney held her breath as Josh snagged the line drive. Before his knees straightened, he reached into his glove for the ball. While her son fired a throw to first, the batter tore down the baseline. One foot on the bag, the first baseman plucked white leather from the air.

"You're out!" called the umpire. "That's the game." Removing his hat, he blotted his forehead on one arm.

Courtney caught Josh's eye. She blew him a kiss and shot him her biggest smile. Hugging Addie to her chest, she grabbed the diaper bag and raced for her car. She'd rolled out the dough for the team's first visit to Coffee on Brevard before leaving for the field. An enormous salad chilled in the refrigerator. Still, she prayed that Nicole had everything else under control.

Dashing into the café minutes later, she swept a glance over the folding tables covered with bright vinyl cloth, noted the sturdy paper plates and plastic utensils arranged in front of each chair. Streamers and balloons gave the place a festive look. Best of all, she inhaled the delicious blend of bubbling Italian sauce and melted cheese atop freshly baked dough. The first of a dozen pizzas were already in the brick oven, with another batch ready and waiting to take their place.

"Hey, Nicole! Any problems?"

"Everything's great, Ms. Smith." Nicole looked up from the pizza she was covering in pepperoni.

"Let me get Addie settled and I'll start on the drinks." She slipped a Baby Einstein program into the DVD she'd temporarily moved into the book nook. Entranced by the puppet figures, Addie plopped down on her well-padded bottom.

Courtney had barely finished placing pitchers of soda and iced tea on the tables when the bell over the door announced the first arrivals. She gave a cheery "Welcome to Coffee *and Pizza* on Brevard" and hustled to take a piping-hot pan from the oven. While the wave of parents and Sluggers found chairs, she checked on Addie. The little girl remained glued to the TV screen.

At least, she did until Travis and Josh arrived.

The minute the coach walked through the door, Addie scrambled to her feet. Calling, "Cosh Oak, Cosh Oak," she toddled to his side. For the rest of the time, while team and family members ate and drank their fill, she eyed the proceedings from the safety of his arms.

At first, Courtney considered rescuing the big guy. Her concerns eased when Addie tugged on Travis's baseball cap. He swung away from his conversation with the catcher's dad to play with her. Her daughter grinned and wrapped her chubby little arms around his neck. The sight spread warmth through Courtney's chest.

Later, after the last of the team and Nicole had departed, Courtney sank exhausted onto a chair. Her jeans had barely brushed the seat before Addie relinquished her stranglehold on Travis. Grinning broadly, she padded across the room.

"Maamaa." She patted Courtney's leg. "Mee-ilk."

"You want a bottle, baby girl?" she whispered. There was one in the fridge upstairs. She made it halfway out of her chair before Travis, his hands filled with plates he'd taken from the tables, stopped her.

"Hold on." He turned to Josh. "Can you get that?"

The boy had just plunked himself in front of the TV set, but he didn't hesitate. He dashed up the stairs.

When they were alone, Courtney turned to the man who apparently had both her children wrapped around his little finger. "Thanks. For everything."

Travis crossed to the trash can, where he dumped the load of cardboard and pizza crusts. "I didn't hear a single complaint. Quite the opposite. Several parents asked if we could make this a regular thing. I told 'em that'd be up to you. You think you broke even?"

That was the question, wasn't it?

"Better," she assured him.

Every pot, pan and bowl she owned had been piled in the sink. The display case had been stripped of every morsel except for two prune Danish. It would take hours to put things right, a full day of baking to replenish the dessert trays. But the till overflowed.

Courtney brushed a few crumbs from her apron. Once the baseball season ended, she could host postgame celebrations for soccer or basketball teams, open the shop for birthday parties on weekends. She'd double-check the books, of course, but her head for business told her a couple of similar events each month would put Coffee on Brevard in the black and keep it there.

She looked up as Josh thundered down the stairs. When she took the bottle he handed her, she paused to give his shoulder a light squeeze. "Thanks, honey. That was some play you made at the end of the game."

"It was awesome, wasn't it?" Josh mimicked the throw.

"Absolutely." Courtney smiled. Two months ago, if anyone had told her she'd praise her son for something he'd done on a baseball field, she'd have thought they'd lost their mind.

She handed the bottle to Addie. The little girl's eyes drifted shut as if a switch had been thrown. Courtney glanced across the room to the man who was responsible for her change of heart, the one who might just have saved her business from going under. Each day, it seemed, the big guy won her over a little more. He possessed every quality she'd ever wanted in a husband, a father for her children. If she wasn't careful, she'd let herself fall in love with him. A prospect that didn't scare her nearly as much as it once had.

Or at least, not as much as telling him all her secrets, including that Josh had inherited his baseball talent from his famous father.

How would Travis react?

He'd probably run, not walk, to the nearest exit.

Not one reporter had listened to her side of the story when the truth about Ryan's affairs surfaced. The media had all but accused her of turning a blind eye on her husband's unfaithfulness in exchange for the big house, the money, the lifestyle of the rich and famous. As for Ryan's teammates and their wives, they'd echoed the party line.

She couldn't bear the thought of Travis treating her the same way, but whether he did or he didn't, the time had come to tell him the truth. The whole truth.

Even if it meant her life would move forward without him in it.

"All that practice you've been doing is paying off."

Travis scooped another armload of paper plates into the trash. "You did a great job anticipating that hit."

"Did you see how I held on to the ball just the way you showed me?" Josh pantomimed the way he'd trapped it in the glove Travis had given him.

Travis chuckled. "I saw it. Now, how 'bout we help your mom out for a little bit?"

Josh spared a quick look over his shoulder. "I'll start there." He pointed to the book nook, where muted voices came from the TV. Grabbing a half-empty cup from the coffee table, he looked around as if he didn't know what to do with it.

"Trash can, Josh," Courtney mouthed.

On her way up the stairs with Addie, she laughed at the way some things never changed. And some changed all too quickly. It wouldn't be long before she'd miss the firm feel of her baby's behind resting in her hand, the sleepy cuddle of Addie's breath against her shoulder. In the tiny room under the eaves, she settled her daughter into her crib.

By the time she rejoined Travis and Josh, the boys had tidied the café. They'd returned most of the furniture to its usual spots. The folding tables they'd borrowed from the rec center leaned against the wall by the door.

"I'll drop these off on my way home." Travis tilted the last table against the others.

"Can I go upstairs now?" Josh pleaded. "The TV down here doesn't get ESPN."

Courtney studied the nook. Neatly stacked magazines stood on the table. Not a single piece of trash remained in sight.

"You don't want to stay down here with us?"

Josh angled his chin toward the mountain of dishes in

the tiny kitchen. A quick eye roll said there were limits
to how much even a boy with a bad case of hero worship
would do for his coach. Josh had, apparently, reached his.

"Okay, shoo." Courtney waved her fingers. "But only
till we finish up down here. After Addie's nap, we'll need
to go to the store." There were groceries to buy if she was
going to restock the display case for Monday.

"Can we stop for a hamburger?"

Peering into Josh's face, Courtney considered the
money they'd made that day. "I think I might have
enough to cover a burger. Maybe some fries."

"All right!" The door at the top of the stairs closed
behind him seconds later.

She turned to Travis. Now that she had him all to herself, she intended to tell him everything. Honest, she did.
But no sooner had her lips parted than his arms wrapped
around her waist and pulled her close. For several long
minutes, she clung to him while he plundered her mouth
with kisses that left her breathless.

When they came up for air, he smiled down at her.
But she couldn't let things continue. She dropped her
hands to her sides.

Emotion swirled and eddied in Travis's dark eyes.
"Don't you want this?" he breathed.

"I—I…" she started.

She didn't know how to finish the sentence. Not if it
meant watching the approval in his eyes turn to disappointment. She slipped her hands into her apron pockets,
where they couldn't roam Travis's broad chest.

"It's okay." He held her at arm's length. "We're going
to take things slow. Neither one of us can afford to make
a mistake."

She took a moment to steady herself before she gestured toward the kitchen. "I guess I'd better get to work, then."

Travis followed her gaze. "You can wash. I'll dry." He grabbed a dishtowel and snapped it in the air. "What?" he asked at her incredulous look. "You didn't think you'd get rid of me that easily, did you? I said slow, not non-existent."

A warm glow put a smile on her face. Maybe if they took things slow enough, she'd find a way to confide all her secrets. Till then she'd concentrate on finding out all there was to know about the man who was impossibly in tune with her needs. She exchanged her soiled apron for a clean one while the sink filled with hot, sudsy water for the pieces that couldn't go into the dishwasher.

"I saw you talking to the Markhams. It looked pretty—" searching for the right word, she paused "—intense?"

"You could say that." Travis shrugged. He wiped the last few drops from a platter. "You know that baseball academy Melinda mentioned? They asked me to write a recommendation for Tommy. They didn't give up easily when I suggested their goals for their son were a bit unrealistic."

Courtney cringed. She could well imagine how that news had gone over with Melinda. "How'd they take it?"

Travis expelled a big breath. "That's one part of coaching I don't particularly like. Most parents are sure their boy is the next superstar. They think their son would be discovered…if only the coach gave him more playing time. Or paid more attention to him. For a kid like Tommy, it's not in the cards."

He lowered the dish to the granite counter. "I tried to help them see that other aspects of the game are just as important. Sportsmanship. Friendships. The ones the boys form now could last their whole lives."

Her brow furrowed. "Do you still have friends from when you were Josh and Tommy's age?"

"Yeah. As a matter of fact, Bob Morgan is one of them. He and I played on the same Little League team. I keep in touch with a few others."

Courtney ran her hands around the bottom of the sink and came up empty. The last dish had been washed. She pulled the plug. Waiting for the water to drain, she asked, "Do you miss it? Pitching?"

Travis polished the last dish until it shone before he answered.

"Coaching helps," he said finally. "And teaching— I enjoy that a lot more than I expected. Helping young boys and girls reach their potential—even if they're not ever going to be professional athletes—well, it means more than I thought it could. I like what I'm doing, even though it won't last much longer."

"You mean when you get that call from the Cannons." She pressed a hand to her fluttering heart.

"Yeah." Travis's brows drew together. "Seems like I've spent my whole life waiting for one call or another."

Courtney blinked and turned away. She'd known almost from the beginning that forever wasn't in the cards for them. Deciding there was no point in telling Travis about her past if they didn't have a future, she wrung out the dishcloth and hung it on the rack.

"Hey, Manny." Travis plunked a couple of dollars onto the plywood counter and withdrew a copy of the local paper. He scanned the front page. A tiny blurb announced the arrival of another cruise ship in Port Canaveral. Unable to stop himself, he grinned. With a boatload of tourists disembarking later in the day, he and Courtney would have Coffee on Brevard all to themselves. With Addie, of course. Not that he minded having the little one underfoot. Truth be told, he liked the way the baby usually reached for him.

Manny slipped the cash into his apron pocket. "There's a right nice piece in there 'bout that new pitcher the Cannons called up from Triple-A."

"I'm more interested in how the Hornets did against the Muck Dogs." He tucked his purchase under one arm. The sports channels kept him up to date on the latest in the major leagues, but the Sluggers and their rivals didn't merit a mention on national TV.

"Hornets by three runs," Manny quipped. "Couple of pictures of your game, too. I think Ms. Smith's boy is in one of 'em." He focused rheumy eyes on the awning that jutted out over the café windows. "I put one aside for her. I was plannin' on takin' it to her in a bit."

"I'm wise to your ways, old man." Travis spread his paper open atop the other stacks. "You just want a cuppa joe."

"You might be right 'bout that," Manny answered while Travis paged to the sports section. Sure enough, a photo of Josh's game-ending play filled one inside corner.

"I'll take every copy you have."

Imagining the excited look on Josh's face when the boy saw his picture in the paper, Travis dug for his wallet. He'd been right about Josh and baseball. The deeper the Sluggers got into the season, the more control the boy demonstrated—both on and off the field. That didn't mean the kid never lost his cool. All boys and girls got angry or upset once in a while. But baseball had been good for Josh.

A spot beneath Travis's breastbone warmed. He'd help turn the boy around. Were there other, equally important aspects of Josh's life he could influence?

Thanks to his mom, the kid had a pretty good handle on opening doors and saying "Yes, ma'am." But respect for women went deeper than that and was best taught by example. Then there were cars. Every boy should learn how to change the oil, to drive a stick. He saw himself teaching Josh how to give a proper handshake.

"Make eye contact," he'd say. "Use a firm grip. One pump. Now two. Okay, smooth release."

And Addie?

His pace slowed. He thought back to how the little girl had clung to him during the last pizza party. No sense denying it. He couldn't have been prouder than if he'd pitched a no-hitter on opening day.

He caught his reflection in the window of a darkened store. His footsteps came to a halt at the thought of putting some pimply-faced teen through the third degree before Addie's first date. The intervening years would pass in the blink of an eye. An urge to be there for every minute of them shook him.

Was that what he wanted? To settle down with Courtney and raise her kids as his own?

He dug deep, demanding an honest answer, and nearly stumbled when he couldn't envision a future without Courtney in it. His breath hitched when he pictured her hair, a wreath of curls on his pillow. Nothing, not even the possibility of coaching in the pros, made his heart stutter like the idea of making love to her. Of waking, his arms snugged around her waist. Of coming home at the end of the day to a house filled with laughter, kids and Courtney.

Oh, yeah, he breathed. If she felt the same way, too, he'd sign up for the whole package, family and all.

But did she?

He straightened the brim of his baseball cap. He didn't know if she realized it, but she had a special smile she saved just for him. Her eyes sparkled whenever they were together. She fit so snugly, so willingly, in his arms that she had to care about him.

On the other hand, he sensed she was holding something back. That there were things about her past she hadn't shared with him. Before they took things to the next level, she needed to trust him enough to tell him what those things were.

He put his feet in motion again. At Coffee on Brevard the usual blast of coffee-scented air washed over him. His attention drawn to the counter, he flashed Courtney his best smile. A split second later, he spied the contingent of Slugger parents crowding the tables. He shook his head. His quiet mornings with Courtney had come to an end, and no one had warned him.

"We'd just about given up on you, Coach. Come on in and have a seat." Larry Olafson, the catcher's father, had the same muscular frame and fair skin as his son. The man pointed to an empty chair between two tables someone had shoved together.

"Catch your breath while I get you some coffee. What do you take in it? Cream? Sugar?" Joe, the father of the team's second-best hitter, was halfway out of his chair by the time Travis laid a hand on his shoulder.

"Don't get up. I'll get it." He hefted the stack of newspapers. "Need to give these to Ms. Smith anyway."

At the counter, Courtney greeted him with a smile that was uncharacteristically cool. "Planning to open a magazine stand, Travis?"

He plopped the papers onto the counter. "These are for you. Josh's picture made the sports section."

Though coffee sloshed against the sides of the pot Courtney held, her expression never wavered. She finished filling his cup as usual and slid it across to him.

"Well, thanks for those." Using her elbow, she nudged the stack to one side. "I'm sure Josh will be thrilled."

He fought the urge to scratch his head. Unless the police were involved, most parents gloated when their child's photo made the paper. The feeling that there was something she wasn't telling him came back with a vengeance. He let his brow furrow. "You don't want to take a look?"

"I'm kind of busy right now." In a deliberate move to change the subject, Courtney threw a pointed glance over his shoulder. "I guess everyone liked the place so much on Saturday they decided to pay us a return visit."

"I should have expected this. During last year's tournament, they all but camped out on my front doorstep. I know you're glad for the business, but—" his voice dropped to a whisper "—I liked spending time alone with you. Is that wrong?"

"Same here." The merest, most reassuring twinkle danced in Courtney's eyes.

Chairs scraped across the floor in the room behind him.

"Better get back." Courtney made a shooing motion. "Your fans are getting restless."

He turned then, the sound of her laughter easing some of his concerns and deepening his disappointment at not being able to steal a kiss or two. At the table, he slid onto the empty chair in time to hear Joe ask, "So what do you think are our chances of going all the way?"

It took every bit of control he'd perfected on the field to steady his cup and keep his thoughts on baseball. He sipped coffee. The scalding brew freed the logjam in his brain and got his thoughts flowing again.

"Baseball players are a superstitious lot," he pointed out. "We haven't lost a game yet, but we don't want to jinx ourselves."

"Heck no, Coach. This is all pure speculation," Joe agreed.

"We just want to be prepared, is all," Larry said, taking the lead in a conversation that covered every aspect of the Sluggers' season.

For the first time in the weeks he'd been stopping by Coffee on Brevard, Travis couldn't wait for the end of his allotted visit. Finally, he gave each of the parents a look filled with one part resolve, two parts encouragement and stood. "Gotta run. See you all at Thursday's game."

A chorus of goodbyes followed him to the front of the café, where Courtney had a coffee ready for Manny.

"See you at practice tonight?" Travis asked, when what he really wanted was to claim a kiss.

"I'll be there. And after that…"

Her voice all but disappeared, tempting him to lean in closer.

"Would you like to join the kids and me for supper?" A rosy glow suffused her face. "My way of thanking you for Saturday." She looked down. Spying the newspapers that still sat on the counter, she added, "And for those."

His body blocking the view of all-too-eager eyes behind him, Travis cupped Courtney's chin with his fingers. "I'd love to," he whispered.

On the way out the door he jingled the change in his pocket, glad for a full schedule and the practice that would eat up the time until he saw Courtney again.

Chapter Ten

Courtney glanced past the chairs and pillows that barricaded Addie in the living room. The little girl sat with a book in her lap and babbled. Josh lay on the couch studying for a test at school later in the week. Satisfied that the kids were out of harm's way, she turned to the stove.

A pork-scented cloud of steam escaped when she lifted the lid from the frying pan. Grease spit and splattered. Once the risk of getting stung passed, she deftly flipped the chops and clamped the lid back in place.

Josh's book closed with an audible snap. "Mom. I'm star-ving," he announced.

Right on cue.

"Dinner'll be ready in just a few minutes. How 'bout setting the table? Knives, forks, spoons, napkins. The works."

Josh scrambled off the couch.

She waited until both his feet hit the floor before she added, "Set an extra place for Coach Oak. He'll be here soon." She noted her son's widening eyes.

"Honest?" His voice rose. "Here?"

She followed as his gaze made a circuit around the room. It wasn't the designer-decorated mansion where they'd once lived. But there were pluses. Josh could build an excellent fort with the well-worn furniture they'd inherited from the previous owners. Addie loved to wiggle her fingers and toes in the yellow throw rug they'd found on sale at the local hardware store.

"You know when someone does something nice for you, it's good to do something for them in return?" At Josh's nod, she explained, "Well, Coach Oak did us a favor by having the team party in the café Saturday. I thought a home-cooked meal would be a great way for us to say thanks."

Behind his easy acceptance, she could practically see her son's thoughts churn. Without saying a word, he padded to the cupboard, where he spent several minutes rattling the silverware in the drawer. When he faced her, she lowered the heat beneath a pot of simmering green beans.

"Mom, if you marry Coach Oak, what's gonna happen to Addie and me?"

Marry Travis?

"No one is talking about getting married." As tempting as that idea was, she shoved it aside.

Tears welled in Josh's eyes. "When Paul's mom got married again, he had to go live with his dad." His chin trembled. "I don't have a dad."

So that's what brought this on?

Fighting her own tears, she wrapped her arms around his shoulders and pulled her stiff little boy close. Paul had lived in their old neighborhood. His parents had been involved in a messy divorce that had led to a bitter custody battle.

"You don't have to worry about anything like that happening with us. I wouldn't want to spend a single day without you and Addie in it." She kissed Josh's hair and, resting her chin on his head, refused to let go until she felt him thaw.

"Mom, I can't breathe," he protested seconds after his hands patted her shoulders.

"So we're good here?" She released her hold, then wagged a finger between them.

In a move that came straight from Travis's playbook, Josh held out his palms. "I guess."

She grinned and swatted his behind. "Good. Now, set the table and wash up for supper." Her thoughts sobered as she turned to the stove.

Josh had changed a lot since the fight at school. He no longer blew up over little things, or even the big things. That didn't mean he was in the clear.

What if he wasn't ready for her to start dating again?

She rested the whisk against the side of the pan. At thirty-two, she was too young to stay true to a ghost for the rest of her life. Even if her first marriage had been a good one, which it hadn't. Not that she'd ever tell Josh how bad things had been.

She shuddered just as the doorbell rang.

Josh called, "I'll get it, Mom." He swung the door open.

Wiping her hands on her apron, Courtney stepped out of the kitchen. She hurried to the entryway, where her son had yet to greet their guest. Over Josh's head, Travis's eyes locked on to hers.

For one second, Courtney let herself get lost in his tender gaze. One second, but it was enough. Standing on the baseball field in a ratty T-shirt and catcher's gear, the man could make her pulse race. In her entryway, droplets of water from a recent shower still clinging to his dark hair, dressed in jeans and a polo shirt, he simply took her breath away.

She caught the scent of flowers and looked down at the bouquet he'd thrust into her hands.

"Those are for you." Travis nodded. He pulled a baseball from his pocket. Handing it to Josh, he said, "It's from the best game I ever pitched when I was in Triple-A. Thought you might like it."

Josh's mouth gaped open. He clutched the gift to his chest.

"What do you say, Josh?" she prompted when her son remained silent.

"Thanks, Coach," Josh whispered. Adulation shone in the eyes that met hers. "Mom, can I put it in my room?"

Travis reached out to mess with the boy's hair. "Good idea. Why don't you."

Josh darted down the hall. As he rounded the corner, Courtney caught the backward glance he cast toward Travis. She knew that look. The boy was trying to figure things out, but he'd have to get in line. Though she'd grown closer to Travis than she'd ever thought she could, he'd as much as said he wasn't looking for a permanent relationship. So where were they headed?

As if answering her question, Travis reached for her the instant Josh sped out of sight. Before she could muster a single objection—not that she would have—he drew her into his arms.

"Better grab a kiss while I can," he murmured. Despite the need that swam in his dark eyes, he brushed his lips lightly over hers.

The teasing touch, the solid breadth of Travis's hand spanning her back, the steady beat of his heart nearly robbed her of coherent thought. She brushed her fingers through his thick hair, reveling in the texture before she drew back.

"Travis," she whispered, "the children."

Addie was too young to notice but Josh—well, if she knew her son, he wouldn't linger in his bedroom long.

"Yeah." Travis trailed one finger along her chin. "Someday, though...."

"I should...I should put these in water." She bent low, hiding her face in the flowers.

"Cosh Oak?" Addie rushed to the end of the barricade and stood there, her little arms open.

Courtney shook her head. "Doesn't look like she'll take no for an answer."

Travis's hand dropped from her waist as his expression shifted into the smile he always wore around her daughter. "Hey there, baby girl." He stepped over stacks of pillows and blankets with an athlete's easy grace. Scooping the toddler into his arms, he pulled another ball from his pocket. "Play catch, Addie?" he asked.

While Josh was busy in his room and Travis played with the baby, Courtney put the finishing touches on dinner. She'd just carried everything to the table when a toddler-toting Travis stepped into the alcove that served as their dining area. Josh skidded into the kitchen behind him.

"Hmm. Something sure smells good." Travis slipped Addie into her high chair. "This looks great."

"It's not anything fancy," Courtney protested. Still, her heart warmed at the way he all but devoured the meal with his eyes.

"Sit here, Coach." Josh pointed to the head of the table. He scooted his own chair marginally closer.

For a few minutes talk died down as plates were

passed. While Josh dove into his dinner, the praise Travis heaped on the simple meal confirmed her suspicions that the big guy subsisted largely on takeout and fast food.

"Careful," she told him when he helped himself to thirds. "Someone might think you're angling for a standing invitation."

The deer-in-the-headlights look she half expected never materialized. Instead, Travis forked the last of the pork chops onto his plate.

"If you cook like this every night, I just might." He peered into a nearly empty bowl that minutes before had held a towering mound of mashed potatoes. "Josh, how 'bout you and I divvy these up?"

"No, thanks." Pushing away from the table, Josh patted his tummy. "Mom, can we have dessert?"

"In a bit." She speared the last of her green beans. "While we wait, why don't you tell us what happened at school today."

When Josh launched into a recitation that started with the moment he stepped out of the house, she dished up brownies and ice cream. She told herself she lost track of the story because her son threw in more twists and turns than a switchback road. Travis, though, interrupted only to ask for more details. When Addie reached for her sippy cup, he handed it to her without so much as a questioning glance.

Josh downed the sweets in record time. He leaned forward, his eyes sparkling. "Hey, Coach. You know why Cinderella ran away with the ball?" His words came in a rush.

Travis squinted. "Are you sure you're telling that right?"

His voice spiraling upward, Josh ignored the question. "Because she got kicked off the baseball team!" He laughed as if he hadn't mangled the familiar joke entirely.

Courtney only shrugged and rolled her eyes when Travis turned a befuddled look her way. Sugar and little boys were a potent mix. Little girls, too, for that matter. Though she'd skipped the brownie, Addie giggled and banged her spoon on her tray.

In quick succession, Josh told three more jokes just as badly as the first.

Travis bumped elbows with the boy. "Hey, kid," he said. "If you ever try out for a part in the school play, we'll have to work on your lines. A lot." He shook his head. "Scary," he mouthed so seriously that Courtney stifled her own laughter behind a well-placed hand.

Happier than she'd been in a long time, she scooted away from the table. "Josh, Addie, time to say good-night."

"Wait a sec," Travis held up a hand. "Don't I get a turn?"

"Yeah, Mom. Coach wants a turn." Josh turned toward the man at the end of the table.

Courtney pretended to object. "I don't know. Tomorrow's a school day. You have to get to bed on time."

"Please, Mom?" Josh begged. "Please?"

"Okay," she answered, trying to look stern and failing miserably. "But just one more."

Travis rested his forehead against a closed fist. "Let me think a minute," he said while Josh all but bounced up and down in his chair. "Okay." He waved his hand. "Okay, here we go. Knock, knock."

"Who's there?" Josh shot back.

"Whoooo's der?" Addie chirped.

"Base," Travis intoned.

"Base who?"

"Base-su?" Addie stifled a yawn.

"Base be getting to bed."

"Good one, Coach," Josh said, his voice echoing the encouraging tone Travis used on the ball field.

"Speaking of which." Courtney gave the clock on the microwave a pointed glance. "Go brush your teeth, Josh. I'll be right there to tuck you in." She scooped Addie from her high chair. The baby waved a sleepy goodbye as she snuggled against Courtney's shoulder.

"How they can go from a sugar high to exhausted in a matter of seconds is beyond me," she said with a tremulous smile that had nothing to do with her children's antics. No, the blame for that lay strictly at Travis's feet. She wondered when she'd fallen in love with him and thought it might have been the moment he'd handed Addie her sippy cup without even giving it a thought. Or maybe it had been when he'd asked Josh about his day and really listened to the boy's story. Or it might have been the first moment she saw him in the principal's office.

No matter when it had happened, she knew only that, against her best intentions, she was hopelessly, helplessly in love with Travis.

Shifting Addie in her arms, she followed Josh down the hall before the truth could escape her lips.

Don't rush it, Travis told himself. This was, after all, the first time Courtney had invited him into her home. Though she pretended the dinner was only to repay him for bringing new business into Coffee on Brevard, they both knew it was more than that. Much more. Maybe the first in a lifetime of meals they'd share right here.

He rubbed his fingers over the scarred wood of a table

barely large enough to seat four. Okay, they'd want something bigger. In a larger place. Someplace like a house with a yard for the kids. With a roomy kitchen where he and Courtney could steal the occasional kiss while they washed dishes or packed school lunches. He pictured a family room with a wide-screen TV he and Josh could watch whenever the Cannons played. One where the toy box didn't serve as the guest chair. A master suite with a king-size bed he and Courtney would put to good use.

Oh, yeah.

Footsteps put an end to thoughts of all the future promised. Josh peered around a corner, his freshly scrubbed face shiny. "Hey, Coach," he whispered. "You wanna see my room?"

Halfway to his feet, Travis slowed long enough to ask, "Is it okay with your mom?"

The boy's head bobbed so fast the action heroes on his pj's shook. "She said you might like to see where I put your baseball while she gives Addie a bath."

Tenderness spread through Travis's chest as he eased the rest of the way out of his chair. At the entrance to a room the size of a closet, he kept his smile firmly in place despite near claustrophobia triggered by sloping ceilings. Gritting his teeth, he ducked his head and took the two steps that put him in front of a shelf above the chest of drawers. There Josh had centered his baseball between several other keepsakes.

"That looks nice." Travis admired a spelling test the boy had aced and a first-place ribbon.

Across the tiny room, Josh climbed under his covers. "You said it was the game ball? Did you pitch a no-hitter?"

"Sure did," Travis answered with a grin.

His head on a pillow, the boy issued a hopeful "Tell me about it?"

Travis snugged the blanket beneath Josh's chin the same way his mom used to do for him when he was a kid. Though the room was so narrow his outstretched legs practically reached the door, he sank onto the edge of the mattress.

"Let's see, it was a Tuesday four years ago." He launched into a tale guaranteed to put stars in a young boy's eyes. "We were on the road again, this time in Newport, Rhode Island. I had no idea I was going to pitch a no-hitter when I woke up in my hotel room that morning...."

While Josh listened in wide-eyed silence, Travis rolled the ball between his fingers and shared the story of his brush with glory. He'd faced his toughest opponents that day and walked off the mound to a standing ovation after seven innings. When he finished recounting the tale, he ruffled Josh's hair.

"Nights like that are what make all the years of practice and hard work worth the effort." He stood, intending to put the ball back where he'd found it. At the shelf, though, he squinted at a faint outline in the dust. Curious, he scanned the room. His focus narrowed in on a wooden bat propped in a corner.

"Was that here before?"

"It's just one my dad gave me." Josh bunched his pillow under his head. "He was supposed to take me to see the Twisters play for my birthday. When he couldn't, he got some of the other players to sign a bat instead."

On his birthday?

The bands across Travis's chest constricted. Small wonder Courtney hadn't wanted anything to do with baseball. Her husband's priorities had been seriously out of whack if he'd attended the game without his son. Travis tamped down a sudden urge to strangle a man who was part of Courtney and her children's history. He ground his teeth together.

He wanted to be their future. To make it a good one.

He crossed to the corner and hefted the bat. "We could make room for both on the shelf, if you want."

"Nah." His eyes drifting shut, Josh yawned. "The ball fits better. Night, Coach."

Travis swallowed past a sudden lump. "Night, Josh," he whispered. He stepped toward the door, his pulse skyrocketing when he spotted the slender form standing there.

"Night, Josh. Love you," Courtney whispered.

"Love you, too, Mom."

Travis's heart beat faster than it did when he rounded third and slid into home. He tiptoed into the hall. While he held his breath and hoped, prayed, he hadn't stepped out of bounds, Courtney brushed past. One finger to her lips, she turned out the boy's light and pulled the bedroom door closed. Though he was pretty sure he wouldn't be able to pry his feet from the spot where they'd rooted themselves, Travis managed to get them in motion when she crooked a finger, beckoning him into the kitchen.

His heart tightened the instant she swung to face him. Beneath the fluorescent lights, tears glistened on her cheeks. The question he'd been afraid to ask faded, unnecessary. She'd overheard enough to make her cry.

Aw, jeez.

"Excuse me a minute, will you?"

She ducked out of sight, leaving him standing there with empty arms and "I'm sorry" on his lips. He heard the sound of water running. He blew out a long breath. When he heard her in the hallway, he summoned a weak smile to cover a sudden uncertainty over what to say next.

"Josh might be one of the best natural talents I've ever seen in baseball, but he can't tell a joke to save his life, can he?"

Courtney's quiet laughter swept away some of his fears. "It's like everything else. He'll get better with practice."

He raised his eyebrows at the unexpected opening. "I can think of other things I'd like to practice." He closed the short distance between them. Tracing his fingers along her jaw, he drew her toward him. A thrill raced through him when she melted against him. His lips found hers and for a few minutes he lost himself in her touch, her taste.

It wasn't enough. No matter how amazing, a kiss never would be. He took her in his arms. When she pressed against him, he gently tugged the band from her hair. He sighed as her curls fell loose about her shoulders. Reveling in the silky strands, he plunged his fingers through them to the nape of her neck. He rained kisses across her cheek, along her jaw, trailed them down to the sweet hollow at the base of her throat. She threaded her hands through his hair and he swore he heard her moan his name when he skimmed his finger along the outline of her curves. Stopping to catch his breath, he wanted nothing more than to kiss Courtney all the way down the hall to her bedroom, shedding clothes as they went. He stared into her blue eyes and saw the same desire in their depths.

He groaned and bent again. A rustling sound came from the baby monitor perched on the kitchen counter.

Reality check.

Reluctantly, he trailed a final series of kisses up to Courtney's lips. Their first time wasn't going to happen tonight. Not in her apartment, where the children could walk in at any moment. He wanted to hear her moan as he kissed her breasts. Wanted to make her gasp. To hear her cry out his name.

And then do it all over again.

And again.

Until they were both utterly and completely spent.

But not in a tiny apartment constructed of thin walls and flimsy doors.

Courtney sighed. Her breath warmed his neck seconds before she slipped from his grasp. Leaning against the counter, her voice far steadier than his own, she peered up at him.

"That thing with the bat… Josh tries to hide it, but he was crushed the day his dad didn't take him to the game." Her voice dropped to the barest whisper. "I can't let my kids get hurt like that again. So, Travis." She paused long enough to fix him with a clear-eyed gaze. "I have to know if you're here to stay…"

He caught the slight quiver in her voice and knew the moment had finally come. It was time to confess he'd fallen in love with her. That he intended to stand at her side for the rest of his life. To be there for all the important moments in Josh's and Addie's lives.

"…or simply passing through," she finished.

All his dreams for the future stuttered. Loving Courtney had consequences, consequences he was 99 percent sure he wanted. Only the tiniest sliver of doubt remained, but it reared an ugly head. *Forever* meant giving up on his dream of coaching in the pros. She might not have shared every detail of her past, but she'd told him enough. Enough to know she'd never settle for an absentee husband or a part-time dad for her children.

But wasn't that exactly what he had to offer?

"I…" He let his hands drop to his sides.

A frown worried Courtney's brow.

"I want to be sure, is all," Travis offered. "You deserve that. They—" he nodded toward the children's rooms "—they deserve it, too."

"But you're not." She sighed.

He couldn't stand to see her hurt, to know he'd hurt her. "It's not you. It's me," he said, meaning the words far more than some trite cliché. "But…"

Courtney held up a hand, stopping him. "But…" She sighed again. "But there's nothing more to say. Not tonight." Confusion swam in the eyes that met his. "I think you'd better leave."

Calling himself all kinds of a fool for risking the best thing that had ever happened to him, Travis forced himself to take the honorable but incredibly difficult steps out her door.

Chapter Eleven

Travis planted his feet well inside the coach's box at first base. A fresh line of sweat broke across his brow. Maintaining an outward calm, he refused to mop his forehead. Late May in Central Florida meant temperatures in the nineties and very little cloud cover, but the heat wasn't responsible for the way his uniform clung like a second skin. No, that privilege belonged to the Sluggers. Down by three runs, their sole chance for the league championship rested on the shoulders of the boy who trudged toward home plate looking as if he'd rather be anywhere else on the planet.

Travis scuffed his foot through the red clay. Would it shatter Josh's confidence if he pulled him out of the game?

He spared a quick glance at the nervous blonde sitting on the third-row bleacher. The way Courtney tugged on her lower lip sent another dribble of sweat down his back. He imagined right about now she was second-guessing every decision she'd made over the past four months.

He squelched an urge to smack his forehead. She and her kids were the best things that had ever happened to him. But as much as he'd wanted to tell her so, when the moment was right, he hadn't been able to choose her over a future with the Cannons.

As it turned out, that future was a whole lot closer than he'd expected.

Last night, the offer he'd been waiting for had been on his answering machine when he got home from dinner. The Cannons expected his answer today and had sent Frank Booker to close the deal. The presence of the man who propped a shoulder against the corner of the snack bar complicated things.

"Two outs. Bottom of the sixth. The Hornets are ahead by three runs. Yes sirree, folks, it all comes down to this. Next up to bat…Jo-o-osh Smi-i-ith." The announcer's voice boomed through the speakers.

Travis forced his head back into the last inning of the last game in the season. A win here would start the Sluggers on the long tough road to the Little League World Series. A loss and the team was done for the year. It would take a miracle and nothing less to turn this one around. With bases loaded and two outs, the boy who'd never stepped into a batter's box before this season would in all likelihood choke. Travis had seen it happen often enough that he refused to put added pressure on Josh. He gave the boy the sign to swing away.

No sense telling him not to. He will no matter what.

Low and outside the strike zone, the ball tore across home plate. Josh swung and missed.

On the visitors' side of the field, parents and grandparents stomped their feet against the metal bleachers. The noise rose to deafening levels.

Travis flashed Josh a confident smile that said it didn't matter whether the boy hit the ball or not.

The pitcher went into his windup. From his vantage

point, Travis spotted the kid's grip and groaned. Looking like every batter's dream, the curveball swirled toward home plate. Travis watched Josh hitch the bat slightly higher. The boy was going to swing.

Swish! Another miss. Strike two.

He caught Josh's look of utter disbelief when the ball spun out of reach.

"No worries." Travis shouted to make himself heard over the crowd. "Just relax and hang in there." Despite the words, his heart shifted into overdrive.

With the count at two-and-oh, the pitcher could afford to throw one outside the strike zone. Sure enough, the ball sailed in high across home plate. Expecting Josh to swing at it the same way he had at tryouts, Travis warned himself not to cringe.

"Ball one," called the umpire.

Behind his sunglasses, Travis's eyes widened. Proud of the boy for laying off the tempting pitch, he gave Josh the thumbs-up sign. "Good job," he mouthed.

The next one barreled down the center of the strike zone.

A resounding crack sent Travis's heart soaring right along with the ball as it reversed course. While the opposing team's outfielders watched in slack-jawed wonder, white leather climbed for blue sky, not leveling out until well beyond the fence. For a moment Josh simply stood at home plate, stunned. Awe filled the look he shot his coach.

Grinning broadly, Travis called, "Go, Josh!" He twirled one finger in the air, the signal for a home run.

Josh dropped the bat and jogged toward first.

One by one, Sluggers tagged up and trotted around the bases, headed for home. One run. Two runs. The third tied the game. When Josh stepped on the plate to score the winning run, the stands erupted. His teammates surged onto the field, where they all but pummeled each other in their efforts to high-five the boy who had saved the day and won the championship.

Even Travis felt his calm demeanor desert him. He sped toward the mob of excited players, wading through them until he spotted Josh in the middle of the pack. Slowing, he nearly choked up as he shook the boy's hand.

"Remember this moment," he managed.

He swept the batter's helmet from Josh's head and lifted the boy high. The kid might never hit the winning run in a game again. The odds were against his ever knocking another grand slam out of the park. But he'd savor this memory for the rest of his life.

At his high school prom, someone would jostle his elbow and ask, "Remember the day you got that awesome hit?" Long after he graduated from college, over beer and burgers at the local tavern his buddies would recall the one that saved the game. "What was the name of our team?" someone would ask, and Josh would smile and say, "The Sluggers."

Travis's chest swelled for the boy who'd come so far in a few short months.

This, he told himself as he lowered Josh to the ground. This was what he wanted to do, what he was meant to do. He wanted to guide Josh every step of the way into adulthood. To help every player on his team, every student in his classes reach their potential.

Whoa, man, do you know what you're saying?

While the team lined up to shake their opponents' hands, Travis's thoughts churned. The position he'd worked for all these years was his for the taking. Did he really want to turn it down? To trade his dream job for a permanent position at Orange Blossom Elementary? To coach Little League for the next ten or thirty years?

One glimpse of Josh's beaming face gave Travis the answer.

He'd spent his whole life waiting. For his coaches to put him into the game. For a call to the Show that never came. For the job offer that finally had. But accepting a position with the Cannons only meant more of the same. Waiting for a call up to the next level, the next team, the next franchise. He was done with it. It was time to start living.

Eager to share his news, he searched for Courtney among the parents who gathered beyond the fence to congratulate the team. She stood apart, not basking in the glory her son had earned. He shot her a V-for-*victory*. She returned it with a cheery wave. But rather than heading his way, she motioned toward the parking lot.

He took a deep breath. One last task remained before he swept the woman of his dreams into his arms and promised her forever.

Travis glanced toward the sidelines where the old scout waited. Brushing his hands on his baseball uniform, he strode toward the man who'd come to the game today with two goals in mind and would leave with only one of them.

In the shade of the snack bar, Frank Booker eschewed the usual handshake to slap Travis on the back. "I don't have to tell you, that was a hell of a game. Hell of a hit."

Travis removed his baseball cap and dusted it on his pants. "Josh has all the makings of a great baseball player."

Frank squinted. "You say he never played before this season?"

"Nope." Travis didn't fault the man for the doubt in his wary eyes. Cheating the system to give a child an extra year or two in Little League wasn't exactly unheard of. He hurried to assure Frank that Josh was the real deal.

"He's headstrong, I'll give you that. Most good players are." Though he trusted Frank to know that success in sports required one part talent, one part determination, a little reminder couldn't hurt. "He's also teachable. The rest of the boys on the team like him."

"Good enough for me." Frank pulled a small notebook out of his back pocket and jotted down a few lines. "That was a gutsy move, letting him stay in the game. Most coaches would've pulled him."

Any guy angling for a job in the big leagues knew the situation called for some assurance that he'd worked out a strategy to win the game no matter what. But Travis's goals had changed. He stared into the distance and gave that rarest of all answers, an honest one. "I wanted the kid to have his moment."

"Oh, that's rich." Frank slapped his hand on one knee. "You save that line. You can trot it out if upper management ever questions the way you handle players in the pros." He sobered. "Like I said on the phone, Jack Madsen announced his retirement. He's leaving at the end of the season. That opens an assistant coaching spot for the Cannons. I'm honored to offer it to you."

Travis took a moment to get his bearings. The money he earned as a teacher was a mere pittance compared to what Frank was offering. But what good was a six-figure salary if it meant never seeing a kid light up the way Josh had today? He looked Frank straight in the eye and said, "Sorry, man. I have to turn it down."

For the first time in all the years he'd known the scout, shock showed on the older man's face. "You've got to be kidding," he protested. "This is what you've worked for ever since you got hurt."

"You're right. It was." Travis lifted his hands in a sign of surrender. "But teaching is what I was born to do. My days in the big leagues are over."

"You won't reconsider?" Frank tapped his notebook against his palm. "You turn this down now, we'll hafta offer it to someone else."

"Go right ahead." Travis scanned the baseball field. A lonely life on the road versus a home, a family and a job doing what he loved. He'd never felt so sure of anything in his entire life. He paused, uncertain whether his decision meant the end of a long friendship.

"You gonna see the Cannons play this weekend?" he asked.

At the scout's nod, he added, "Saturday is Little League Day at Twister Stadium. If you want, I'll introduce you to Josh's mom. Make sure she understands you'll do right by her boy." Courtney wouldn't let her past stand in the way of Josh's chances for a career in baseball, not after she learned an honest-to-goodness pro scout had shown an interest in her son. He met the older man's inquisitive gaze.

Frank tipped his hat. "I'm flattered that you think so highly of me, Travis."

"Yeah, well, don't let it go to your head." He bumped shoulders with his old friend. "I aim to keep a close eye on the boy, too."

Minutes later as he hustled toward his Jeep, Travis

considered his next step. Maybe he'd go back to school, get his master's and become a principal. Maybe he'd continue to teach P.E. Whatever he did, he knew for sure that bringing out the best in young boys and girls would be as much a part of it as Courtney, Josh and Addie.

He couldn't wait to make the commitment that only a few short weeks ago he'd resisted with all his might.

THE MOMENT SHE spotted the wizened figure near the snack bar, Courtney's stomach performed a series of flips guaranteed to put an acrobat in the Cirque du Soleil to shame. She veered away, heading for Travis's car instead of the dugout, where she'd planned to meet Josh. On her way she risked a single glance over her shoulder.

No doubt about it. That was Frank Booker, all right. When Ryan had been at his peak, they'd attended the same parties, moved in the same social circles. She hadn't seen the man in ages, but anyone even vaguely associated with major league baseball knew the Cannons scout.

So what had brought him to a Little League game?

Her back to him, she forced herself to breathe. Just because he'd shown up at the field the same day her son hit a grand slam, that didn't mean he'd make the connection between Josh and his infamous father. Still, a tremor of unease passed through her at the idea that Frank might connect the dots the way no one else had.

Though she dreaded the pitying looks, the raised eyebrows that were sure to follow, she'd always known the truth would come out sooner or later. Before that happened, she wanted to tell Travis all her secrets.

Would his feelings change when he learned them?

She pulled the brim of her baseball cap down low. She

couldn't be certain how he'd react. Not after the way he'd bolted for the door last night.

Leaning against his car, she rubbed her fingers over a tender spot just below her breastbone. They'd agreed to take things slow until they were both sure, but her chest ached every time she thought of a future without him in it. Picturing the bear hug he'd given Josh at the end of the game, she sighed. Travis was exactly who she wanted in her life, in her children's lives.

But did he want her in his?

Cleats scraping across blacktop put her troubled thoughts on hold. Their arms slung around one another's shoulders, a group of Sluggers crossed the pavement with her son at their center. Josh looked so happy that tears tickled the back of Courtney's throat.

Refusing to embarrass the Boy Wonder in front of his pals, she raised her hand to give him a high five.

Ommph!

She struggled to stay upright when her sturdy young boy broke from the pack and slammed into her.

"Did you see it, Mom? Did you see my hit?"

Gathering her wits along with her balance, she wrapped her arms around her son. "Yep. I sure did." Love and pride warmed her heart as she stared into his upturned face. "It was awesome! I'm very proud of you." Only a few months ago such praise would have been impossible in more ways than she could count. She swallowed a fresh onslaught of tears and kissed the top of his head.

"We won!" Josh broke free. Unable to stand still, he danced around her.

She blinked, her eyes misty despite her efforts. Those first few months after the move, she'd been so afraid for her boy. But the sullen stranger had disappeared. In his place stood an excited, happy young man tapping an impatient foot. She gave him a playful nudge.

"I'll see you at the café in a little bit." She studied the boys who were riding together to Coffee on Brevard. "Now, don't you eat all the pizza. Save a slice for me. And two for Coach Oak."

A chorus of "Yes, Ms. Smith" nearly drowned out Josh's "I will. Thanks, Mom. See you later."

Watching her son and his friends dash off toward the waiting vans, Courtney marveled at how much their lives had changed. Business at the café was on the upswing now that the parents from Josh's team had discovered it. The weekly phone calls from his teachers focused more on her son's achievements than his problems. As for Addie, she shook her head. She could scarcely believe her baby had become a toddler. In another year, Addie would start preschool. And after that, kindergarten. Courtney checked her watch. She and Travis would pick the youngest Smith up from her first playdate on their way to the pizza party.

No doubt about it, the decision to come to Cocoa Village had been a good one.

Glancing toward the bleachers that had quickly emptied after the last out, she spotted the man who played a pivotal role in her family's happiness. She skimmed Travis's muscular frame and felt a wash of emotions. Thanks to him, she'd developed a new appreciation for baseball. He'd taught her it wasn't about competition and backstabbing. He'd shown her that the camaraderie the boys felt, both on and off the field, was an important part of the game. And if he asked, she'd let Josh play as long as Travis was willing to coach him. Still amazed at her change of heart, she smiled up at the man responsible for it.

Nearing her, he swung a look at her side. "Where's our little hero? Waiting in the car?"

"He went on with the Markhams. I called Nicole, warned her to expect a gang of ravenous boys." With Coffee on Brevard on firm footing, she'd hired the girl's sister to help out with the weekly pizza parties. "Sounds as if they're on top of things."

Travis's footsteps slowed. "You mean I have you all to myself?"

"Rare times," Courtney said, pointing out the obvious.

She wasn't sure what to think when he slipped an arm around her shoulders out in the open, where anyone could see. Her breath caught when he brushed a kiss across her lips. She gave him a gentle shove.

"Travis, what if someone notices?"

He only pulled her closer. "Let 'em," he growled. "I've been wanting this all day. Haven't you?"

She spared a sidelong look at the man, who only last night had shied away from any sign of commitment, yet now held on to her as if he wouldn't mind if the whole town saw them together. The change sent a shiver of anticipation down her spine. Almost afraid to ask, she whispered, "What's up?"

Above his sunglasses his eyebrows quirked. "I'd say we need to talk, but someone else already stole that line."

Thinking back to the day she'd spoken those very words sent another delicious shiver through her. Even then she'd known she was falling for him. She glanced at the few cars left in the parking lot and decided that if Travis didn't care about them, she wouldn't either. She brushed a kiss against his cheek.

"So what *is* up?" she asked again.

"Frank Booker stopped by to watch the game. You might have seen him? Wiry guy in a dark blue hat? He scouted me in high school and college. We've kept in touch through the years."

"Oh," she managed. She felt the world shift into slow motion as she waited to hear that Frank had recognized her. Or worse, shown an interest in Josh.

"He said Jack Madsen is retiring at the end of the summer."

She heard the seriousness in Travis's voice, felt it in the chill that brushed her shoulders when his arm dropped to his side. Her stomach tightened as he turned to face her.

"Jack's departure opens a slot for an assistant coach in Norfolk. Frank offered me the job."

"Oh! That's…"

Her heart plummeted, taking her dreams of a future with Travis along with it. Love or no love, she couldn't uproot Josh and Addie, not when they'd finally adjusted to their new life. To say nothing of Coffee on Brevard. Give up all she'd worked so hard to achieve in order to follow Travis to the first in a series of new cities, new jobs? Try to build a life together while he was constantly on the road with the team? She couldn't. She wouldn't. She tried to extricate herself from his embrace. He held her in place while he traced one finger down her cheek.

His tone solemn, he said, "I turned him down, Court."

"What? Why?" Despite his hand on her shoulder, she stumbled. Her voice caught. "That's your dream job, what you've always wanted."

"You're right." Travis moved into the space her retreating feet had vacated. "I've always thought if I couldn't play in the Show, coaching would be the next best thing."

She frowned, the thousand reasons why she'd promised she'd never fall for another baseball player lodged in her throat. "You know how I feel about—"

He waved a hand, cutting her off. "Josh needs a dad who'll be there when he gets up in the morning. To tuck him in when he goes to bed at night. And for all the hours in between. Addie, too."

He paused while her heart tripped over itself, then said, "I want to be that kind of man."

As much as she thrilled at his words, she backed up another step. Sadly, she shook her head. Her hands against his broad chest, she maintained the space between them. "I can't let you walk away from your dreams. Not for me, for us. What if things don't work out? You'd blame me. I don't think I could bear that."

He surged into the space between them as if some unseen force propelled him.

"I won't lie. You're a huge part of the reason I turned it down. But not all. I love what I'm doing right here at Orange Blossom. I love working with the players, helping them achieve their potential. The kids in P.E., I'm trying to instill in them habits that will last a lifetime."

Uncertain, she studied the ground. "You're very good at what you do. Everyone, from Bob Morgan right on down, says you're a great teacher." She pointed to the field behind them. "Any kid lucky enough to have you for their Little League coach knows the same thing."

"Besides," Travis continued, "coaching in the pros is no kind of life for a family man."

Almost afraid to believe what she was hearing, she lifted her gaze. Through a shimmer of tears, she studied his serious expression. She had to ask. "Are you planning to become a family man, Travis?"

Lips made for kissing curved into a teasing smile that lightened the air, making it easier for her to breathe.

"I hear some gorgeous blonde with a headstrong boy and an adorable little girl has an opening. I thought I might apply for the job." He wrapped one arm around her waist and pulled her close. "I think I have the inside track. I'm tight with the owner."

"You don't think it's too soon?" she whispered. "I mean, we haven't known each other that long and..." She closed her mouth, shutting off the useless protests.

She'd known the moment she'd first laid eyes on him that he was special. Everything he'd done or said since then had only bolstered that impression. But it was too soon. Too soon to admit she'd fallen head over heels in love with him. She felt for her poor ragged composure and made the smart decision to say how much she liked him. What came out instead was "I love you, Travis."

In an instant, she was pressed against his chest, listening to the strong beat of his heart.

"I was hoping you'd say that. I love you, too. I don't think I can go another day without you in my life. I want to prove that to you." His hand swept against her curves. "In oh-so-many ways."

At his touch, a bolt of white heat shot straight through her midsection. She sucked in a shaky breath. "Yeah. Me, too," she whispered.

"So we're good, then?" he murmured. "I'll stay on here at Orange Blossom. And we'll get to know one another better?" He rained light kisses along her neck. "Much better?"

Wondering how they'd been so lucky to find each

other, she trembled beneath his touch as they walked the short distance to his car. There she couldn't resist the urge to bury herself in his arms again. Intending to steal only a single kiss, she splurged on a dozen. And a dozen more after that.

He smelled of spring, the outdoors and his own uniquely masculine scent. She drank them in, opening to him as she'd never dared before. His love swept away the last of her reservations. She moaned his name when his hands slipped beneath the hem of her T-shirt. She guided her own over his uniform, relishing in the flex of muscle beneath the fabric. She kissed him until she couldn't last another minute without the feel of his skin against her own. Breathless, she pulled back.

Okay, she admitted. Maybe it had been a little more than a kiss. Her breath came in little sips and her insides quivered. Thinking of what she'd like to do next and where they were expected to be, she groaned.

"We should wait," Travis said as if he'd read her mind. "The team and their parents are already at the party. We can't skip it."

"Tonight Josh is having a sleepover," she said, nearly regretting her promise to let him invite a friend to spend the night. "Tomorrow we'll have a long day at Twister Stadium."

"But after that…" Travis leaned in for another kiss.

When she could speak again, she agreed. "Yeah, after that."

Chapter Twelve

Courtney shimmied into a pair of cargo shorts. Smoothing fabric that had softened after a season of twice-weekly washings, she tugged a faded Sluggers T-shirt over her head. She scrutinized her image in the mirror. Highlights she'd easily afforded as the wife of a superstar had long since faded. Though her finger and toenails glistened, the pink polish came from a bottle she'd picked up at the grocery store. These days she toned her figure at Coffee on Brevard rather than an upscale spa. Even her face had changed over the past year. Gone was the slightly bemused expression she'd perfected as the de facto leader of the Twisters Wives' Club. In its place she wore a genuine smile.

Would anyone at today's game recognize her?

Doubtful. But to be sure, she propped oversize sunglasses atop her cap and slipped her feet into flip-flops the wife of Ryan Smith wouldn't have been caught dead wearing. Courtney Smith, owner of a café in downtown Cocoa and girlfriend of Travis Oak, didn't have such pretensions…and she'd never been happier.

Tonight, after they returned from Twister Stadium, she and Travis would go out on their first real date. The thought sent a thrill of anticipation through her. She could hardly wait to spend the night in his arms.

Her pulse thrumming, she called, "Josh, are you ready?"

Heavy footsteps trudged down the hall. His shoulders rounded, her son stepped into the room still dressed in his pajamas.

"Mom, my stomach doesn't feel so good."

She eyed the boy who'd had no trouble putting away three pancakes and an extra helping of bacon less than an hour earlier. He didn't look sick. Sad, maybe, but not sick. Her heart sank a little.

"Come here, honey."

She pressed her palm against his forehead. "No fever." She hadn't expected one, not really. She folded herself around his solid little frame. "Are you thinking about your dad?"

Josh buried his face in her shoulder. "I don't know," he mumbled. "I guess."

"It's hard not to on a day like this." She combed her fingers through hair that needed a trim. "You probably miss him, huh?"

Josh only burrowed deeper into her arms. "I think I'm s'posed to. But he wasn't like my friends' dads. He was always yelling about something."

Well, there was that.

She patted Josh's shoulders. "That wasn't your fault. Or mine. Your dad, he pushed himself to be number one all the time. In any profession, that's a good goal. If you work really hard at it, you might get to be the best for a while. Sooner or later, though, someone younger or stronger will come along and take your place. That's tough for some people to handle. It was for your dad."

She braced for the anger that usually rose whenever she dwelled on her past with Ryan. To her surprise, she felt only a wisp of regret, proof that she'd grown, had changed enough that she no longer needed to hold on to the old hurts. She rubbed Josh's shoulders and hoped he wouldn't either.

"You got that, buddy?"

"I think so," he said slowly. His face scrunched. "After Dad, after he…you know…none of my friends wanted to hang out with me anymore. Do you think people here are different?"

She swallowed past the insults and betrayals her little boy had suffered. "I think your new friends appreciate you for who you are and not because you're the son of somebody famous. I'd like to think that Coach Oak is right. He says they'll be your friends for always."

"I'd like that, too," Josh murmured.

Sensing the crisis of the moment had passed, she gave him a final squeeze. Like her, Josh had done a lot of growing up since they'd moved to Cocoa Village. She tickled his ribs. "Why don't you get ready so we can go."

She watched her son race down the hall. A few minutes later she held Addie close, inhaling her little girl's sweet scent while she went over instructions with the babysitter. Her insistent toddler clamored to get down, and Courtney sighed. The days of cuddling her baby were numbered.

Did she want another one?

A baby? The question caught her off guard, and she almost laughed.

How many nights had she walked the floor alone with Josh? Or rocked Addie until dawn when she couldn't sleep? A dozen? A hundred? Did she really want to go through all that again? Would Travis?

The image of a tiny newborn resting on his wide chest shushed her objections. Maybe another baby wasn't such a terrible idea. Not with Travis at her side. She kissed her little girl's cheek and lowered her to the floor.

"Give Mama a goodbye hug," she said as Josh headed downstairs, where he'd probably con Nicole out of a snack from the display case.

"Bye-bye." Addie waved. She turned toward her stacking toys. "Bewuuu." She picked up a blue ring and slid it onto the pole.

Courtney fluffed the child's curls and followed Josh.

At McLarty Park, the boy practically bolted from the car the minute he glimpsed the three large tour buses that sat in the parking lot, their engines idling. Travis waited for them, too, just as she'd known he would. He stopped Josh, clapped the boy on the back and sent him toward the first bus.

In spite of his dark sunglasses, she knew Travis's eyes shone just for her. His full lips curved into the smile she'd come to expect whenever he looked her way.

Certainty flooded her. Here was the man she wanted to spend the rest of her life with. The man she'd entrusted with her heart, her family.

On its heels came the question she'd avoided for too long. Would he forgive her for the secrets she'd kept? He deserved to hear the truth from her own lips, and she decided to tell him everything, the whole truth. Now. Before they left for Twister Stadium.

Opening her car door, she stepped into his embrace. He leaned into her. "We still on for tonight?" he whispered before he kissed her.

"Can't wait." She already wished the day was behind them. "You have a minute?"

"For you, all the time in the world. What's up?" He waved an absentminded greeting at the cars that pulled into the rec center's parking lot.

One glance at the players and parents who had arrived earlier than expected and Courtney knew she'd missed her chance. Her news would have to wait until she had Travis all to herself.

"It's probably nothing, but Josh said his stomach hurt this morning," she hedged.

"Gotcha," Travis said, steering them toward the buses. "We'll make sure he limits himself to three hot dogs and two bags of popcorn."

That much junk food wasn't exactly the cure she'd been hoping for, but the seriousness of his tone told her she could trust Travis to watch out for her son.

The next two hours passed in a flash as she and Travis checked names off lists, made sure everyone boarded the right buses and squelched the occasional prank during the fifty-mile ride to Orlando. Walking into Twister Stadium brought a fresh flutter of unease, but she kept her head down, her chin tucked into her chest, while the Sluggers paraded around the field with teams from all over the state. She hung back while Travis introduced his players to the starting lineup for the Cannons and the boys got autographs.

She breathed easier when they finally headed for their assigned seats. High on the upper deck, she sank onto a wooden bench next to Travis. For a while they stayed busy, passing bags of peanuts or popcorn, hot dogs or sodas down the line of hungry young boys. Soon that tapered off, leaving them free to watch the game. Which, as far as Courtney was concerned, didn't compare to the sensation of Travis's bare knee next to hers, her hip pressed to his, his arm oh-so-casually draped across the back of her seat.

But it was a bad day for Twisters fans as the Cannons piled up runs in the first six innings. They scored twice more before their first baseman hit into a double play to retire the side. In seconds, ticket holders surged to their feet for the seventh-inning stretch. As the visitors headed for their dugout, the strains of "I'm a Twister, you're a Twister" reverberated through the stadium. Cameras zeroed in on toe-tapping fans who had forgotten, at least temporarily, that the other team was winning.

Courtney glanced up at the images displayed on the huge monitors and pulled her baseball cap low over her eyes. Far below them, the Cannons ran onto the field while the Twisters prepared for their turn at bat. And then one last picture flashed onto the JumboTron.

Beside her son, his pals nudged and pointed as Josh's face filled the huge screen. Laughing, he pointed to his image while the announcer's voice played through the sound system.

"Ladies and gentlemen, let's give a warm Twister welcome to Josh Smith. Josh is here today with his Little League team, the Cocoa Village Sluggers. I hear Josh hit a grand slam yesterday to win the championship. Sounds like he's following in his father's footsteps. Yes, that's right. Josh is the son of the late Ryan Smith, the greatest hitter in the history of baseball. So let's give it up for one of our own."

The stadium erupted, though not everyone was as pleased as the announcer to have the late superstar's family in their midst. Courtney froze at the catcalls and boos that punctuated the applause. White noise filled her head. People pointed, fired questions. She couldn't make out the words, couldn't respond if she'd wanted to.

She didn't.

Her gaze locked on to her son. Surrounded by his pals on the next row down, he seemed oblivious to the jeers that sounded so loud in her ears. All grins, Josh's teammates bumped shoulders with him and traded high fives. Once the applause faded, Josh grabbed his bag of popcorn and went back to watching the game. She knew there'd be more questions, more issues to deal with later. For now, though, he'd handled his newfound notoriety in typical kidlike fashion.

Certain that Travis, too, had heard the crowd's reaction and would finally understand why she'd kept her past a secret, she turned to him.

The man beside her had turned to stone.

Aware that the arm across her shoulders had grown rigid, she swallowed a sour taste.

"Travis?" she whispered.

He waved her off. His jaw worked. A harsh whisper meant for her ears alone hissed across his lips. "Ryan Smith, *the* Ryan Smith?"

Her heart in her throat, Courtney could only nod.

Travis stood, his expression shuttered. Without so much as a second glance, he stepped into the pedestrian tunnel that led to the main floor.

A shudder ran through her. She had to explain. Had to tell him that keeping her secret had nothing to do with him and everything to do with shielding her family from the media. From pitying looks and accusations. From people who condemned her for putting her children's needs above her own.

She signaled the assistant coach to watch the boys and took off after the man she wanted in her life forever.

On the mezzanine level she caught a glimpse of his broad shoulders just before Travis ducked into the men's room. Her feet skidded to a stop outside the door. Ten minutes later she was still waiting when Frank Booker strolled into view looking as if he'd won the lottery. Apparently, tearstained cheeks were no deterrent to the scout. He walked straight up to her and held out his hand.

"Ms. Smith, it's good to see you again." His perpetual squint narrowed. "You must be so proud of your son. I know the Cannons will be following his development very closely. Travis was sure right when he said the boy could play. He's the image of his father."

Courtney's heart stuttered. She drew herself to her full five feet two inches and stared the man straight in the eye.

"How is Travis involved?" she demanded.

"Why, he invited me to come see the boy play." The scout bared his yellow teeth in a grin.

Okay, so she hadn't told Travis everything, but from the moment they met, she'd made her feelings about baseball abundantly clear. *That* was one thing she hadn't kept secret.

A fresh round of tears swarmed into her eyes. Anger helped her battle them. Certain of only one thing, she scrubbed her cheeks. No matter what his motives, no matter what his reasoning, Travis had gone behind her back to do something he knew she adamantly opposed. "Mr. Booker, I'm afraid you've been misled. Josh isn't going to play professional baseball. Not ever. Now, if you'll excuse me."

Her chin wobbled but she refused to let another tear

fall. Instead, she began counting the hours. One more at the stadium. Two to load everyone onto the buses and drive back to Cocoa. Addie would have long since gone to sleep by the time she got home, and Josh, Josh was staying with the Markhams. That made three hours, four tops. She could hold it together that long. But after that, there was a heartbreak waiting with her name on it.

Courtney and Ryan Smith? *The* Ryan Smith.

Like a missed grounder, the news bounced between Travis's feet. Needing time to come to grips with such an earth-shattering idea, he sought the privacy of the men's room. The sounds from the noisy stadium faded as he propped his hands on either side of a sink. He let his head hang low enough that none of the other guys would notice the moisture that gathered in his eyes. Moisture, he insisted, because P.E. and Little League coaches didn't cry any more than former minor league baseball players did.

No wonder Josh showed a lot of promise. With Ryan Smith as his father, the boy probably had more natural baseball acumen in his little finger than Travis had in his entire body. And he'd tried to coach the kid?

Just give him a bat and let him swing, fool!

As for Courtney, things made a lot more sense now that he knew she had once been married to the greatest hitter who ever lived. He groaned, thinking of how he'd tried to impress her with his own prowess at the bat. She'd never been dazzled by his skills, and why would she be? Her husband had been the best of the best.

His mind racing, he thought back to the blue dress she'd worn to the Little League fund-raiser. He'd thought then the gown clung to her curves as if it'd been made for her. It probably had been. Some fancy designer in New

York or Paris had in all likelihood crafted it precisely to her petite form.

He swore softly. She probably had closets full of the things.

After all, she'd lived in the rarefied world of a superstar. She was used to elegance and fancy restaurants. While the best he could offer were casual dinners at the local pizza joint.

He shook his head. She deserved better. Better than a second-rate pitcher. A washed-up has-been who'd traded his cleats for a career as a teacher.

The sudden urge to smash something buzzed about his head. His hands fisted. He reared back, stopping himself only moments before his knuckles shattered a mirror.

He flexed his fingers.

There was more to Ryan Smith than his history in baseball. If only half the tabloid accounts were true, the man had been an abysmal father, a loathsome husband. His hair-trigger temper on the field was as legendary as his batting statistics. Any other player would have been benched. Maybe suspended. Instead, according to locker-room scuttlebutt, the front office had hired a PR company to cover up the affairs, the DUIs, the gambling.

No wonder Courtney didn't trust baseball to do right by her son.

But she hadn't trusted him, either.

When Travis got down to the heart of the matter, that was where it all fell apart. She hadn't trusted him. Not enough to tell him who she really was. And without trust, how could there be love?

Motion behind him made him check the mirror. The bathroom had grown crowded, the way it usually did at the end of an inning. No matter how much he wanted to crawl home and howl, it was time to get back to his team. He splashed cold water on his face and retraced his steps through the tunnel.

Right where he'd left her, there sat Courtney. Despite her shocking revelation, she hadn't even cared enough to come after him but sat, her arms crossed, her knees pressed tightly together, looking anywhere but at him. He slid onto the bench, careful not to brush against her.

His stomach hit a new low as he waited for her to apologize. Or at least explain. She did neither, instead offering him a cold shoulder and a healthy dose of the silent treatment. He endured it longer than any sane man could. Midway through the visitor's last at bat, his eyes glued to the action on the field, he issued a slant-sided whisper. "Why didn't you tell me?"

"What difference did it make?" Cold air brushed his shoulder when she gave an indifferent shrug. "Ryan's gone. Besides, I'm not the only one who kept secrets."

"You know everything there is to know about me." Travis cupped his hands over his knees.

She turned to him then. Not that it helped. Dark sunglasses hid whatever emotion filled her eyes.

"I thought I did. I trusted you. I trusted you with Josh. And you betrayed us." There was no mistaking the angry tremor in her voice. "You spoke to Frank about him."

He wanted to challenge her accusation, but couldn't. He had contacted Frank. Had praised the boy's skills. If he'd known the truth about Josh's father, he might have acted differently. But he couldn't change the past. He bit back the attempt to justify his actions with a shrug that asked, "Why bother?"

Someone had to say the words, and he thought it might as well be him.

Straightening his hat brim, he kept his voice soft. "I think we should cancel our plans for tonight."

She merely nodded. "Fine by me."

And with that, his heart twisted, his mind finally catching up with the fact that things between them were over before they'd even gotten started.

"I'll trade places with one of the other coaches for the ride back," he offered. He sent a pointed look over the line of Sluggers, who'd won their local championship. After another week of practices, they'd face their first opponent on the road that might lead to the Little League World Series. "Should I find a new team mom to finish out the season?" He let the question dangle.

Courtney followed his gaze. "I won't let the Sluggers down," she said, her tone resigned. "But I can handle the details without your help."

Tonight, after they returned from Orlando, after the boys dispersed to their homes, after he stowed the gear and pulled into his own driveway, then he'd let himself think about a future without Courtney or Josh or Addie in it. For now, such thinking was too dangerous. Too risky. Too apt to bring about a decidedly unmasculine reaction. And so Travis crossed his arms, leaned back in his seat and prayed for the agony of the day to end.

Chapter Thirteen

"She's all right? No fever? She hasn't thrown up?" Checking in with the babysitter, Courtney stared over the steering wheel at the ball field where the Sluggers would play in their first postseason tournament. Should she go home? Should she stay? She struggled with the choice the same way she'd second-guessed every decision since she and Travis had called it quits.

"No, Ms. Smith. Addie only picked at her lunch, but we played pat-a-cake and read books until it was time for her nap. She went right to sleep."

Courtney wavered. Her gut insisted that the fussiness this morning had been a sign of bad things to come.

Or was that just an excuse to avoid Travis?

The thought of seeing him again so soon after their disastrous trip to Twister Stadium sent her heart into free fall. Yes, she should have told him about her oh-so-famous first husband from the very beginning. Or at least the minute she realized the attraction between them went deeper than a passing interest.

So, yeah, she accepted part of the blame. Not that the breakup was all her fault. Far from it. But no matter how many sleepless nights it took to put her heartbreak behind her, she couldn't take one step further into a relationship that had no future. Which was exactly what she and Travis had—no future.

"I'm five minutes away. Call me if there's any change," Courtney said, slamming the lid shut on all thoughts of a certain Little League coach. She stepped from her car at McLarty Park and spotted Josh warming up in the infield with the rest of his team. There was no sign of Travis, and she told herself that was a good thing.

Most likely, it'd take a lifetime before she made it through an hour, much less a day, without yearning for his strong shoulder to lean on. Till that happened, she'd keep moving forward. For today, that meant working in the snack bar, where she could watch the Sluggers play without risking a run-in with their coach.

For a while, a long line of customers kept her busy. So busy she barely noticed that Travis sported several days' worth of facial hair and looked pale beneath his tan. Or that the Sluggers trailed by three going into the sixth and final inning of what looked like a very short tournament season. Or that the scouts in the stands tracked Josh's every move like a flock of vultures.

She stopped bagging popcorn when Josh's name came over the loudspeakers. Her stomach tightened when she spotted her boy on his way to the pitcher's mound. She homed in on the Sluggers' dugout, forced herself to make eye contact with the one person she'd spent the game avoiding.

Travis locked in on her gaze.

"I'm sorry," he mouthed.

For what? For counting on my son to save the game? Or for betraying my trust?

She swallowed the unanswered questions when Josh went into his windup.

His first pitch sailed so high over the batter's head the umpire didn't even bother to call the ball. Courtney studied her son for any sign of anger, but he simply shrugged off the bad pitch and concentrated on the next one. In quick succession he delivered two strikes before the batter popped up to the second baseman.

It should have been an easy out, but the boy dropped it. Despite the error, Josh managed to hold the other team to one run in the inning. Still, that put the Sluggers down by four when they came to their final at bat.

Courtney surveyed the crowded stands. Slugger fans cheered. Mothers in green jerseys hugged one another and prayed. Agitated fathers walked the fence line, hoping their sons would make miraculous hits to save the game and send the team on to the next level.

But the first three batters struck out. Game over. All hopes of a district or state title dashed.

Disappointment pricked at Courtney's eyes. Slowly, she began dishing up snow cones while the dispirited Sluggers shook their opponents' hands at home plate. Afterward the team headed for the shade trees, where she had no doubt Travis would help them cope with defeat the same way he'd never let winning go to their heads.

She had nearly finished with the tray of icy treats by the time snippets of a heated conversation drifted through the snack-bar window. She paused, holding the ice scoop aloft when she heard her name.

"I'm telling you, the Smith woman knows how the game is played. She'll move to Miami if it gives her son a better chance to turn pro."

"You couldn't be more wrong," countered the voice that had disturbed her sleep all week.

She froze, straining to follow the exchange above the

general hubbub of people placing orders and the sound of cola flowing into cups.

"Look," said Frank Booker, "there's not a doubt in my mind this kid's got what it takes. But he needs the right program. You and I both know a couple of seasons in Little League won't be enough."

Behind her, corn popped furiously in the kettle, nearly drowning out Travis's "Give the boy a chance to grow up, will ya? He needs time, stability. He's getting that here."

Frank's voice grew more insistent. "What he *needs* is a coach who eats and sleeps baseball. Nothing but baseball. By the way, how are his grades?"

Courtney could practically see Travis scuff a foot through the dirt before he answered.

"Improving. He'll do even better next year."

"Down in Miami, they'll make sure he sails through his classes. He'll have all the time he needs to concentrate on what's important."

How dare they!

Courtney let the scoop fall into the bin. Intending to put a stop to the two men blithely discussing *her* son's future, she firmed her shoulders.

"Your plan won't work."

Hearing the same firm assurance that had molded an inexperienced boy into a key player on the Sluggers' team, she slowed her steps.

"Josh doesn't want to play baseball. He wants to act. As a matter of fact, I hear he's signing up for drama class next fall."

Josh?

Courtney felt her eyebrows rise. Much as she loved her son, even she had to admit the boy couldn't deliver a punch line if his life depended on it. Something Travis knew full well.

She sped out of the snack bar. Rounding the corner, she spied the two men, their arms crossed. She noted the firm set of Travis's jaw and wondered if Frank had any idea that he'd gone up against a formidable opponent. One who didn't give up on the things he wanted.

But did he still want her?

"Mr. Booker," she announced, "we need to talk."

The scout frowned while the tiniest smile played at the corners of Travis's lips.

"Ms. Smith, I only—"

"Hold it right there." Courtney held up a hand the way she'd seen Travis do on the field. "Let me be clear. One day, when he's old enough, Josh can decide for himself about his future. Whether he wants to follow in Ryan's footsteps. Or do something else."

She cast a glance at Travis. Understanding flickered in his dark eyes. She stilled when he leaned down to whisper in her ear.

"Are you sure, Courtney? You don't have to do this. Josh doesn't have to play baseball. Not ever."

Frank tried to interrupt. "I only want the best for your son. Why, down in Miami—"

She cut him off. "There'll be no talk of moving. Of finding Josh another coach." She sought Travis's eyes. "I've made my choice."

Looking down at her, Travis's face filled with the same longing she knew her own held. She drew in a shuddery breath and tore her gaze away. Frank had taken a step back, but the scout still stood close enough to hear her low warning.

"And one more thing. Spread the word, Mr. Booker.

The first representative who approaches me—or my son—gets a permanent black mark by their name. Have I made myself clear?"

"Crystal." Frank pointed, his finger moving back and forth between Travis and her. "Looks to me like you two have other things to discuss. I'll leave you to it."

She had to give the old scout credit for recognizing a lost cause and wondered if she was fooling herself. Just because Travis had taken her side, had taken Josh's side, that didn't mean there was any hope for them, did it? Her pulse pounded. She had to learn the truth before it was too late.

The shouts and cheers of people in the stands, the smell of hot dogs and popcorn and peanuts—they all faded. Her focus zeroed in on the man who stood in front of her.

"Do we, Travis?"

TRAVIS SCRUTINIZED FRANK'S departing back. A small voice inside his head said he should walk the man out to his car, smooth the scout's ruffled feathers. His heart overruled such foolishness. He mopped his chin with his hand, felt the bristle of a beard he hadn't bothered to shave since he and Courtney had called it quits.

The petite blonde peered up at him. Sorrow and something he was afraid to name shimmered in her blue eyes. The fact that she'd consider the prospect—no matter how remote—of Josh ever playing professional ball, well, that was nothing short of amazing. But it didn't compare to the idea that *they* still might have a future together.

He removed his baseball cap, ran a hand through his hair. His fingers came away damp, but then, Courtney had always had that effect on him. His mouth refused to form the question he really wanted to ask: *Do you still love me?* He reached for a safer topic.

"How are things at the café?"

"Busier than ever," she said, though the tiny space between her brows deepened. "I was afraid business would drop off when you stopped coming by in the mornings. Guess I underestimated the local gossip mill." She gave a mirthless laugh. "There's always a silver lining, no matter how bad things get."

Travis's chest tightened. "No one's pestering you, are they? 'Cause I'll…"

His voice died. Until he knew how involved he'd be in her future, he wouldn't make empty promises.

"No one's said a word, at least not when I'm around." A wistful smile played over Courtney's lips. "Manny and the other shop owners have made it quite clear that anyone who has a problem with me will have a problem with all of them, too."

Travis pictured the spry octogenarian at the newsstand taking on a bully. If he were a betting man, he'd put his money on the eighty-year-old scrapper. "That's the beauty of small-town life," he said. "We take care of our own."

"And where does that leave us?"

Direct, to the point. He liked that about her.

She stared so hard at him he practically felt her scour his face. His heart constricted. He wanted nothing more than to wipe her doubts away and spend the next fifty years with her.

"Courtney, I contacted Frank so long ago it surprised me as much as anybody when he showed up the other day. But I was wrong to call him. I know that now."

Her soft "He told me" raised more questions than it answered.

"When?" he asked.

She stared into the distance, a hint of heartbreak in her eyes. "At Twister Stadium. After they flashed Josh's picture, I followed you. I knew I should have told you about Ryan earlier. I tried to that morning, remember?"

He shut his eyes. At the time, he'd suspected there was more to the conversation than Josh's upset stomach. A knot loosened somewhere in his chest, and his breath came easier than it had in a week.

"Bad timing," he murmured, thinking of the arrivals who had interrupted their talk.

"Yeah," she agreed.

He could have let it go at that. Could have chalked up the whole heart-wrenching episode to bad timing, bad information. But he had to clear the air between them. Wanted her to know he'd learned his lesson. He scuffed one foot. "I let you down. And for that I'm sorrier than you'll ever know."

Her response surprised him.

"You don't owe me an apology." Hesitantly, she reached for his arm. "I'm not blind. I know Josh inherited Ryan's talent, his drive. To tell you the truth, it scares me to death."

He hooked his thumbs on his pockets to anchor his hands in place.

"I spent a lot of sleepless nights worried about him... until you stepped into our lives." Her words tumbled out in a rush as she brushed away the tears that tracked down her cheeks. "Let's face it, you mean the world to Josh and Addie."

As much as his heart thrilled to what he was hearing, as much as he wanted to be a permanent part of her children's lives, it wasn't enough. It never would be. Putting everything he had into the most important pitch of his life, he asked, "So if I were to ask, you'd give *us* another chance?"

"More than a chance." Her eyes widened until he thought he could see the very depths of her soul. The emotion he'd glimpsed earlier was back, and this time she put a name to it. "Travis, I've never loved anyone the way I love you."

Her declaration called for a kiss and he was just the man for the job. He stepped forward. Promises filled his mouth, his heart.

Footsteps crunched on the gravel-lined walkway. Courtney's cell phone pinged. The sights and sounds of a park filled with young baseball players and their families rushed in just as Josh rounded the corner of the snack bar.

"Everybody's waiting for you, Coach."

Timing. It was all about the timing.

He turned to Courtney. "I have to give the team a pep talk."

She waved her cell phone. "The babysitter."

"Ask her if she's free to watch Addie and Josh tonight. I'd like to take you out to dinner. Maybe a little dancing."

"You looked real good out there today, slugger." Whistling, Travis settled a hand on Josh's shoulder a few minutes later.

"We lost, Coach. I lost the game."

Travis shook his head. "It takes nine men to win or lose, son." He liked the way that last word felt on his tongue and gave the boy a squeeze. "Sometimes you just have to wait for your chance to start over. That's what we'll do next year."

It was what he and Courtney would do. Beginning tonight.

He judged the distance to the trees where the rest of the team waited. Deciding there was time, he leaned a little lower.

"There is something I want to talk to you about. Man-to-man stuff."

Josh straightened, and if Travis didn't know better, he'd swear the boy's chest puffed out a bit. He fought to keep a smile out of his voice.

"I…um…I like your mom. A lot," he admitted.

"Yeah, I got that." Josh treated him to a world-class eye roll. His footsteps slowed to halt. "She's been crying a lot. She hardly ever cries. Did you have a fight or something?"

Travis hung his head. A long breath seeped through his lips. "We did. But we made up."

"So you're gonna be friends again?"

He wasn't about to tempt fate by asking a ten-year-old for his mother's hand.

"Well," he said, keeping things simple, "I'd like us to be more than that. I want to spend a lot more time with her. And with you and Addie. Would you be okay with that?"

One of the longest minutes in Travis's life passed while Josh rubbed his chin and thought the matter over.

"Yeah, but…" Uncertainty clouded his young voice. "I already had a dad."

"And no one could replace him, Josh. I'd never try. But I'd like to be a part of your life, yours and your sister's. If your mom agrees."

His words matching his pace, Josh slowly put his feet in motion. "Addie's too little to remember him."

Travis glimpsed the man the boy would become when Josh gave a solemn nod.

"I think she needs a dad," he said at last.

Damned tears. They clogged his throat, forcing him to clear it.

"What about you? You need someone to stand behind you no matter what?"

"As long as you make Mom happy again, I'm good."

Someone who didn't know him might mistake Josh's slightly lifted shoulder for an evasive shrug. Travis caught the sheen of moisture in the boy's eyes and knew it was more than that.

"You sure are," he agreed, clapping Josh on the back.

As for making Courtney happy, he'd do his very best.

Later he barely recalled the talk he gave the team. Oh, he knew he'd spoken with each boy, praised this one's hitting and that one's fielding. Told 'em to practice hard so they'd be ready for next year.

But he couldn't remember a word he'd said.

No grand slam, no shutout, no triple play had ever felt as good as hearing Courtney say she loved him as much as he loved her. Now that he knew how she felt, he didn't want to wait. Not to make her his. Not to let the world know he was hers. Driving home, he dreamed of the life they'd build together. The house they'd buy. The yard with the white picket fence. The two kids they'd raise as a team. The others they might one day add. In all the ways that counted, he'd made it to the major leagues after all.

He shook his head to clear it. He was getting ahead of himself.

A stop in downtown Cocoa put him on track. Though

his cleats left a trail of red clay across the polished tiles, the jeweler's knowing smile only deepened as he helped Travis choose a heart-shaped diamond from the display. Weighted down by the small box in his pocket, he dropped by the florist's before he headed home.

Three hours later, shaved, showered, dressed in his best khakis and polo, he stood on the landing of the apartment over Coffee on Brevard. One hint to Melinda Markham had resulted in an invitation that Josh spend the night at Tommy's. Travis brushed damp palms against his pants. He and Courtney had dinner reservations at Café Margaux, where the understanding maître d' had promised a table in a quiet alcove. The champagne was on ice, his delivery down pat.

Would she say yes?

Cellophane crinkled as his grip on the bouquet of flowers tightened. She'd once kept Tiffany's on speed dial. The city's finest chefs had catered her dinner parties. Would she consider his efforts paltry by comparison?

Steady, boy. The past was behind them. The future lay ahead. He knocked on the door.

He blinked, momentarily taken aback, when Courtney answered wearing the same Sluggers T-shirt she'd worn at the ball field.

"I'm sorry, Travis." She bounced a squalling child at her hip. "Addie has a fever. I think she's coming down with something."

A ninety-mile-an-hour fastball takes one half second to cross home plate. In less time, Travis's plans changed.

"No problem," he said, dumping the flowers on the entryway table. "We'll stay in. I'll take Addie. You take a break."

"I could use a shower. You sure you don't mind? You look all spiffed up."

Seeing the glint of appreciation in her eyes, he rubbed his hand over his freshly shaved chin. "There'll be other nights." The future held no guarantees. It made no promises, but he was sure about one thing. Whatever it held for them, they'd embrace it together. He smiled and reached for the baby.

"Okay, then." Courtney ran a hand through her curls. "I'll just be a little while."

"Take your time." He reached into his back pocket for his phone. A hefty tip would bring their dinner to them. "The food won't be here for at least an hour. Meanwhile, me and Addie, we'll hang out."

He settled into the rocker with the wailing baby. He tried to give her a bottle. She pushed it out of her mouth and cried harder. Gently, he patted her backside to no avail. Finally, he put her against his shoulder and crooned to her while the realization of what it meant to be a father started to sink in.

Was he up for this?

More than, came the ready answer.

The muffled sound of running water, the one lullaby he knew by heart and the rhythmic motion of the rocker finally did the trick. Addie's wails faded to soft hiccups. Within minutes, she slept against his shoulder, her warm breath tickling his neck. He waited until he was sure she'd fallen sound asleep before he settled her in her crib. Carrying the monitor, he returned to the living room just as Courtney emerged from the back of the apartment.

Damp tendrils curled loosely about her perfect face. She'd slipped into the fancy dress he liked, the one she'd worn to the fund-raiser. He cracked a grin at her bare feet, glad she'd lost the painful-looking sandals.

He closed the gap between them.

"I've been waiting for this moment for such a long time," he whispered.

He kissed her then, the first brush of his lips against hers stirring a fierce hunger. He swept the tip of his tongue across her mouth, and she opened to welcome him. He tasted mint and inhaled the sweet scent of her perfume mingled with the faintest hint of soap. As their tongues met, he plunged his hands into her hair the way he'd dreamed of doing for as far back as he could remember. He threaded his fingers through the silky strands and moaned her name.

Wanting, needing, to do things right, he tamed the fire before it could engulf him. He caught the uncertainty that flared in Courtney's eyes. Softly caressing her hand, he dropped to one knee. He slipped the box from his pocket the way he'd practiced.

"Courtney, I'm not the greatest catch in the world, but I love you more than life itself. Will you do me the honor of becoming my wife?"

A sudden attack of nerves wasn't part of his plan. The world tilted on its axis, the small box trembling in his outstretched hand as he waited for her answer.

COURTNEY'S HEART STILLED. A soft "Yes, oh yes" barely escaped her lips before she tugged Travis to his feet, unable to wait another second to have his arms around her, his mouth on hers. Her hands shook as he slid the ring onto the third finger of her left hand.

"If it's not what you want…" he began.

She shushed him. "It's perfect," she insisted, catching

the brilliant sparkle in the light. "But you're even more perfect." She tipped her head then, and time stopped as she lost herself in a kiss she never wanted to end.

An hour later, breathless and hungry for more than kisses, they were still wrapped in one another's arms when a knock sounded at the door.

"Take-Out Taxi," came a voice on the stairs.

Courtney sighed. "Do we have to eat?" she asked, peering up into Travis's eyes.

Gently, he kissed the tip of her nose. "Stamina, woman. If we're in this for the long haul, I need sustenance."

"Well, then, by all means." She grinned then and, looking down at her rumpled clothes, ducked around the corner.

"Hold that thought," he whispered before crossing the door to pay the boy.

Later, as they traded bites of the baked brie and portobello mushrooms that were the restaurant specialty, Travis asked, "Have you given any thought to where and when you might like to become Mrs. Courtney Oak?"

Her cheeks warmed as she considered how they'd spent the last sixty minutes. "You haven't given me much time to make wedding plans," she whispered.

"I was thinking maybe before school starts in the fall?"

She gave him a doubtful look. "Half the town will want to be there. Most places book up months, sometimes years, in advance."

Travis spread soft cheese on a toast point. "What about holding the ceremony at McLarty Park? We could stand at home plate and say our vows."

She blinked, unable to hide her skepticism. "I admit

my feelings for baseball have changed. But for our wedding?"

He sat so close that she felt his laughter before she heard it. Her lips curved as she sighed. "You were teasing me."

The admission earned her another of Travis's amazing kisses. When they broke apart, he gazed intently into her eyes.

"Where doesn't matter. Not to me. Not as long as we're together," he insisted. "But I don't want to wait. Not a moment longer than we have to."

"I do happen to own a café." She closed her eyes, picturing the banisters of Coffee on Brevard draped in tulle.

"Perfect," Travis declared. A stricken expression crossed his face. "Unless you want something fancier. A big reception. With waiters in tuxedos and a live band. I know that's the kind of thing you're used to. We could do that, if you want it."

"I don't need fancy," she whispered. "I just need you."

She loved the feel of Travis's hands as they slipped around her waist, his breath against her neck when he leaned in to steal a kiss. Slowly, she eased her plate onto the coffee table, much preferring Travis's embrace to anything even the finest restaurant had to offer. Not so long ago, she'd had all the trappings that came with wealth and fame, but that life had been empty, vacant. For a while she'd thought she'd lost everything. Instead, she'd found true happiness, love and a second chance for her family in the little town of Cocoa Village.

Knowing she'd made the right choice, Courtney sighed into Travis's kiss.

* * * * *

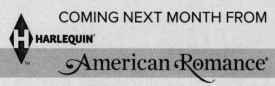

COMING NEXT MONTH FROM

HARLEQUIN

American Romance

Available March 4, 2014

#1489 THE TEXAS WILDCATTER'S BABY
McCabe Homecoming
by Cathy Gillen Thacker

Environmentalist Rand McCabe embarks on a passionate affair with lady wildcatter Ginger Rollins, but can't convince her to begin a real relationship with him...until she finds herself unexpectedly pregnant with his child.

#1490 MOST ELIGIBLE SHERIFF
Sweetheart, Nevada
by Cathy McDavid

Ruby McPhee switches places with her twin sister so she can lay low in Sweetheart, Nevada. She doesn't expect complications—except it turns out Ruby is "dating" Cliff Dempsey, local sheriff and the town's most eligible bachelor!

#1491 AIMING FOR THE COWBOY
Fatherhood
by Mary Leo

An unexpected pregnancy hog-ties Helen Shaw's rodeo career and friendship with future father Colt Granger. The sexy cowboy's proposal sounds sweet, but is it the real deal?

#1492 ROPING THE RANCHER
by Julie Benson

Colt Montgomery has sworn off women after his ex left him to raise his teenage daughter alone. When actress Stacy Michaels shows up at his ranch, she tests his resolve to steer clear of women!

————————

YOU CAN FIND MORE INFORMATION ON UPCOMING HARLEQUIN® TITLES, FREE EXCERPTS AND MORE AT WWW.HARLEQUIN.COM.

HARCNM0214

REQUEST YOUR FREE BOOKS!
2 FREE NOVELS PLUS 2 FREE GIFTS!

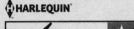

LOVE, HOME & HAPPINESS

Ruby McPhee is hiding out in Sweetheart, Nevada, having changed places with her twin sister. What her sister didn't tell her is that Scarlett was dating the town sheriff! But what happens after Cliff Dempsey figures this out? Find out in MOST ELIGIBLE SHERIFF *by Cathy McDavid.*

Picking up the bouquet, Cliff said, "These are for you."

"Thanks." Scarlett accepted the flowers and, with both hands full, set them back down on the table. "You didn't have to."

"They're a bribe. I was hoping you'd go with me to the square dance Friday night."

The community center had finally reopened nearly a year after the fire. The barbecue and dance were in celebration.

"I…um…don't think I can. I appreciate the invitation, though."

"Are you going with someone else?" He didn't like the idea of that.

"No, no. I'm just…busy." She clutched her mug tightly between both hands.

"I'd really like to take you." Fifteen minutes ago he probably wouldn't have put up a fight and would have accepted her loss of interest. Except he was suddenly more interested in her than before. "Think on it overnight."

"O-kay." She took another sip of her coffee. As she did, the cuff of her shirtsleeve pulled back.

He saw it then, a small tattoo on the inside of her left wrist resembling a shooting star. A jolt coursed through him. He hadn't seen the tattoo before.

Because seven days ago, when he and Scarlett ate dinner at the I Do Café, it hadn't been there.

"Is that new?" He pointed to the tattoo.

Panic filled her eyes. "Um…yeah. It is."

Cliff didn't buy her story. There were no tattoo parlors in Sweetheart and, to his knowledge, she hadn't left town. And why the sudden panic?

Scarlett averted her face. She was hiding something.

Leaning down, he smelled her hair, which reminded him of the flowers he'd brought for her. It wasn't at all how Scarlett normally smelled.

Something was seriously wrong.

He scrutinized her face. Eyes, chocolate-brown and fathomless. Same as before. Hair, thick and glossy as mink's fur. Her lips, however, were different. More ripe, more lush and incredibly kissable.

He didn't stop to think and simply reacted. The next instant, his mouth covered hers.

She squirmed and squealed and wrestled him. Hot coffee splashed onto his chest and down his slacks. He let her go, but not because of any pain.

"Are you crazy?" she demanded, her breath coming fast.

Holding on to the wrist with the new tattoo, he narrowed his gaze. "Who the hell are you? And don't bother lying, because I know you aren't Scarlett McPhee."

Look for MOST ELIGIBLE SHERIFF *by Cathy McDavid next month from Harlequin® American Romance®!*

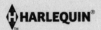

American Romance®

She gave in to temptation—again!

Environmentalist Rand McCabe embarks on a passionate affair with lady wildcatter Ginger Rollins, but can't convince her to begin a real relationship with him…until she finds herself unexpectedly pregnant with his child. How long can he keep his feelings—and their baby—a secret? Rand vowed to love and honor Ginger forever. And it's a promise he intends to keep….

Look for
The Texas Wildcatter's Baby
by CATHY GILLEN THACKER

from the McCabe Homecoming miniseries
next month from Harlequin American Romance.

Available wherever books and ebooks are sold.

Also available now from the McCabe
Homecoming miniseries by Cathy Gillen Thacker

THE TEXAS LAWMAN'S WOMAN
THE LONG, HOT TEXAS SUMMER
THE TEXAS CHRISTMAS GIFT

www.Harlequin.com

HAR75510